TWENTY SIX LETTERS

TWENTY SIX LETTERS

JANE M MEADOWS

This edition published 2023 by:
Takahe Publishing Ltd.
Registered Office:
77 Earlsdon Street, Coventry CV5 6EL

Copyright © Jane Meadows 2023

ISBN 978-1-908837-30-1

TAKAHE PUBLISHING LTD. 2023

For my Daughter

In this world where we live there should be more happiness
- and for me - because of Rachel - there is.

About the Author

Jane Meadows lived in Kenilworth for many years and now lives in Coventry where much of the book is set. She has been writing for as long as she can remember and although she has had several poems published this is her first novel. She was inspired to publish after her daughter read it and loved it. And also by a quote she read on a tea towel in a beach bar in Ferragudo. Part of which said:

Aged 60 she looks at herself and reminds herself of all the people who can't even see themselves in the mirror any more, and goes out and conquers the world ...

Contents

Introduction

Many years ago, 15 or more, an old friend of mine came to my door with a carrier bag full of letters. He had been helping a neighbour clear out her garage following the death of her husband. When he'd asked her what she wanted him to do with the letters she simply said, get rid of them. I don't think giving them to me was quite what she had in mind but give them to me he did.

I glanced at them and then put them in a shed and forgot about them. Over the years some got damaged, some got nibbled by mice and some just faded completely. During the dreadful days of Covid, whilst looking for something to do, I took took them out and when I counted the remaining readable letters there were exactly 26. What a great title for a book I thought.

So I read through the letters and was intrigued by the contents. The original owner had long passed and I haven't used the actual letters, names or places but did steal a few ideas and thoughts from them before respecting the the lady's wishes and 'getting rid of them'.

I had some dear friends that met in a similar way in 1939, as did my own parents and it got me thinking about how resilient the human race is, that in the face of such turbulence, and the horror and tragedy of war we still have the ability to look to the future even though we are not even sure there will be one.

So it is a simple story of hope really, and of love. If you read no further than this introduction then so be it, but if you do go further I trust you will enjoy reading it as much as I have enjoyed writing it.

Jane M Meadows
September 2023

Letter One

68 St Andrews Rd
Cheltenham

28th May 1939

Dearest Fred

Somehow I don't want to write to you, I just want to shut my eyes and think about you, hearing your voice when you just spoke to me so short a while ago. It's absolutely no good trying to write to you the thoughts and feelings that seem to fill my mind. It's at times like this when you have just left that I realise how much you mean to me. You believe me don't you dear? I saw you go past in your coach, it was raining hard and you didn't see me, but you were looking out of the window and I knew you were looking for me. I got quite a thrill out of seeing you although it hurt to think that you were going away. You know I believe that happiness and pain are closely related – somehow, when one is most happy it is quite possible to feel pain. For instance, just before you left do you remember asking me if I was crying? Well, actually I wasn't, but I could have done so quite easily but I was also feeling very happy. I was in your arms, the best place to be in my opinion. Fred, I wish you were here now to hold me in your arms, I could go to sleep quite happily! Anyhow, I'll have you to think about and I know you will be thinking about me, you will tonight won't you dear?

I suppose I must go to bed now – I guess mother must think I'm a "trifle fond of you" I have you most of the day, and as soon as you've gone I commence writing to you, perhaps in thinking so she is correct, do you think so? Oh dear I must say goodnight dearest, but I'll still be thinking of you.

I will continue, It's Monday now, I've just been swimming and have arrived home dripping water from my golden locks – I'm getting very hardy because it's frightfully cold here today, I'm thinking of going swimming again tomorrow – don't you wish you could come dear? I've just looked through the previous part of this written last night, it may strike you that I am rather soft, I hope not, but I'm afraid that I felt that way last night. There was a lovely moon, I got out of bed and watched it and wondered whether you had reached home, I hope the journey didn't tire you out dear? You know it was frightfully sweet of you to come all that way for such a short time to see me, it rather mystifies me that you can care enough for a person like me to do things like that. I do hope you don't really think I'm a child, because really I'm not, I don't think that you do because if you did I don't think you would like me.

Just think dear, in less than a week you will be with me again, I do hope dear you will be able to get down as easily as possible. If you remember you could bring some worms and some string – we could extract minnows and sticklebacks as you wanted to yesterday, you must have been a nice little boy, but a bit on the devilish side, at least I should imagine so. I think it was settled that you should come down next weekend, taking that for granted, I think I should convey, through you, my thanks to your mother for suggesting that I should visit you the following weekend, perhaps you could thank her nicely for me, and explain, would you? I really must close now or I shall miss the post – I do hope that you are not working too hard, please write back nice and soon won't you? I'll be expecting a letter, a long one please – I know you would hate to disappoint me!

Goodnight dearest Fred

Your very own

Joyce

Fred was on his second cup of coffee when the post arrived, he knew immediately it was from Joyce, his mother knew as well, she smiled to herself, but it was a tight smile that didn't quite reach her eyes. She finished clearing the table whilst Fred played with the letter, turning it over in his fingers, he sighed quietly and stood up from the table, scraping his chair back and tucking the letter into the inside of his jacket pocket. His mother turned from the kitchen sink and raised an eyebrow in his direction "aren't you going to open it son?" she asked, "'no time" said Fred trying to sound more carefree than he felt. "Its bound to be a long one, I'll save it until I get home tonight". He shrugged into his coat and straightened his tie in the small mirror by the door, kissed his mother on her cheek, and turned to leave "Goodbye mum, I'll see you this evening, I shouldn't be late, but I'll let you know if I have to do any overtime" – a sideways grin and he was gone. Mrs Osborne finished tidying the breakfast things away and reflected on how so much can change in such a short time, she worried about Fred, she really did, and now he'd got himself involved with a young girl who lived miles away. With so much unrest in the world she wondered if it was wise. Still, what could she do, he was a grown man now and there were worse things that could happen, much worse.

Fred Osborne was just shy of his 30th birthday, he lived with his mother in a suburb of Coventry on a pleasant, tree lined avenue, although the house was terraced rather than detached the area was considered a little upmarket, and indeed in years to come would be much sought after and very expensive. He didn't consider himself upper class by any means, in fact possibly not even middle class, but that's what other folk would say. He had a good job in the city as head clerk at a reputable firm of accountants and often thought himself to be reasonably lucky. Considered by his friends to be an all round good egg, whatever that's supposed to mean, he was just the right side of handsome, had a good physique and an easy going way with the opposite sex that made them feel comfortable in his company.

He had felt, up to a couple of weeks ago, that his future was fairly well mapped out for him. He had been courting a young local girl called Irene for a few months and although nothing had been said there was a kind of understanding, most who knew him thought that he was ready to settle down and maybe, possibly, almost certainly, an announcement would be made on or before his birthday. It was assumed that his new wife would move into the family home, at least it was by his mother, and that his life would be comfortable and content. He wasn't a particularly ambitious man, his job wasn't too taxing although sometimes the hours were long, he had a close circle of old friends whose company he enjoyed almost daily, and most of all he was a good son who loved his mother. And then a week in Skegness changed everything for him, just as everything was about to change for everybody, the timing couldn't have been more inconvenient.

Letter Two

68 St Andrews Rd
Cheltenham

12th June 1939

My dear Fred

Thank you so much for my letter which I received this morning, I'm frightfully sorry that you have got a blister, it was frightfully selfish of me to drag you all that way without thinking of your comfort, next time you find me doing anything like that, please tell me off – a lot. The thing was Fred, I was so frightfully happy to have you here that I'm afraid I couldn't think of anything else. Also I'm sorry to hear that you have got a bad hand, it was sweet of you to write to me when it hurts you so. Reading your letter I realise that you seem to have found it difficult to write to me, it doesn't seem like you, rather stilted, this is rather funny to me because I'm quite sure that I could write to you about anything now.

This letter has got to be the nicest one that I have ever written to you, because I intend you to get it on your birthday, after all you must be happy on that day mustn't you? How I wish I could come and spend it with you, we could have quite a celebration couldn't we? I expect your mother will make a fuss of you on that day – I'm sure I shall feel quite jealous. Fred dear it seems ages since Sunday, it seemed quite desolate when you had gone. I just hated having to let you go, I didn't seem to have said half the things that I wanted to tell you. I do hope you enjoyed it half as much as I did, you know, it has been worrying me these last few days to realise just how much I do care for you, I'm quite sure that it's lots more than is good for me. Still, one doesn't arrange these things – they just happen don't they? After all it was a mere trick of fate that we both happened to have been in Skegness at the same time, and also that we managed to meet up with each other quite by chance. I often try to reason out why all these things happen, why certain *things, which seem most unlikely to occur do, and on the other hand why people (usually the best people) have to be hurt. Fred dear I do hope you won't suddenly change your mind and stop caring for me – I'm sure I couldn't bear it.*

I seem to be writing rather morbidly to you, I must apologise (I feel rather like I could cry my eyes out, I don't know why). Enough! This is supposed to be a joyful epistle. Fred dear, do you like roses? We've got simply sheaths, I nearly sent you some which I had given to me, and then I thought, you send girlfriends roses, but hardly boyfriends. Have you got many flowers at your home? Perhaps your mother would like some roses (that's if you haven't any) Oh I do hope you will be able to spend a few hours with me on Sunday (I'm getting selfish again I'm afraid). Of course it's ok for you to let me know on Saturday morning. I will meet you anywhere you say if you come, if not I will ring you at 11am, ok?

Its unfortunate that your 'Best Man' affair interferes with your holiday, I should imagine that you will make an excellent Best Man! Kissing all the bridesmaids etc, still, I think your friend ought to realise that in the first place you are doing him a favour, anyway, I expect you will fix it up somehow, I hope you are trying! Are you? A former friend brought mother round some music – the pile contained 'One day when we are young' When its played I promise you my thoughts will be with you. Dear, I hate to think of you being a 'martyr' to write to me when it hurts you so – you know quite well that I should understand – still, I love you for doing it, I'm glad you don't get your secretary to write your letters, it consoles me a lot.

I'm filled with remorse for dragging you all over the place and causing you to get a blister – I promise to behave better next time. If I don't you can always tan me! It might do me good and you have my full approval. You know I didn't realise you had it in you to tease people so, perhaps I am an easy victim, I'm getting to know you ever so well now. By the way, you seem to like saying "How are you?" I can hear you saying it time and time again, I can just imagine the tone of your voice as you say it!

> *Dearest, I hope you like the wallet, I'm afraid I know very little about such things, you see I'm not in the habit of buying males birthday gifts, so please accept it – understanding that I send you all my love with it. A very happy birthday my dearest.*
>
> *Your very own*
>
> *Joyce*

This time Fred had opened the letter straight away, he had been expecting it, looking forward to it even, but at the same time dreading it, he knew that a decision was going to have to be made soon, It was quite clear to him as he had read through the 'epistle' that Joyce was under the impression that the decision had already been made. It shouldn't have been so complicated, Joyce was a delightful, lovely, funny girl that any man would be happy to have on their arm, he had got himself into a real pickle this time. It wasn't the distance between them, although that wasn't ideal, but that she was such a child, a ten year plus age gap was ok when one was in their thirties and one was in there forties but she had only just turned nineteen and he just turned thirty, which made him feel rather old and think of her as rather young. It had all seemed like so much fun when they had met in Skegness, Fred had been staying at the rather exciting Butlin's holiday camp with some friends giving Tom, a last hurrah before he got married and Joyce had been staying in a guest house with her mother, her younger sister Elsie and Joyce's best friend Rachel. They met when they had all been walking on the promenade, Fred and his friends were heading for the fun fair and Joyce and Rachel were laughing and taking photographs of one another with a Kodak brownie. He had stopped and offered to take a picture of them both and the upshot was that they all ended up going to the funfair together.

It should have all been so easy, they only had a few days and then they would go their separate ways, a holiday romance if you will, often joked about, but up until now never experienced, but they seemed to spend an awful lot of time together in those few days. What he didn't realise was how taken Joyce was with him, and he had to admit, she was a delightful companion, quick to laugh and so excited about life and the world and everything in it, she had an innocence about her that was a breath of fresh air in these uncertain times. That Joyce was infatuated with him went completely over his head until his pals started to rib him about it and all at once it was only too obvious, he should have let her down gently there and then but something stopped him and when she suggested that he might care to visit her in Cheltenham the following weekend he found himself agreeing. He badly wanted to see this charming young woman again.

By this time Joyce's mother knew about the dashing young man she had met on the promenade and she also had her misgivings but knowing her daughter as she did she wisely kept her own counsel, for the time being anyway, no doubt expecting that little would come of it.

So he had set out on a rather grey Sunday morning and taken the coach down to Cheltenham, Joyce had been extraordinarily thrilled to see him, and as it happened, he was quite delighted too. She wore her blonde hair down and looks as pretty as a picture. They went to her home where he was introduced to her mother, who shook his hand politely but otherwise said very little. In all fairness there was very little time to say anything at all, Joyce hustled him out of the house as soon as was polite and they spent the next few hours walking and talking. Amazingly, he felt very at ease in her company, she definitely brought out the best in him, he felt so relaxed with her that the time flew by and they only just made it to the coach station for him to catch his ride home, it was raining by then and when she lifted her face to his it was impossible to tell if she was crying or not as he held her in his arms, he hoped not, but he couldn't be sure.

When he had arrived home his mother was sitting in the kitchen waiting for him, to his relief she didn't question him, just asked how it had gone, and if he was ok. Feeling that he had to give her something. Fred said he didn't know if he wanted to talk or not, but at least now he felt that he knew what needed to be done, he decided to sleep on it and think about it again tomorrow when he would make a decision. His mother seemed satisfied with this, "you're a grown man Fred" she said "and a good one, whatever you decide will be the right choice for you".

The conversation Fred had with Irene the following evening did not go well, but a darn sight better than he had expected. Irene was a sensible girl and wasn't about to fall to pieces in front of him, she told him he was a fool, that it was only a holiday romance, that the girl was too young for him, all of which was true, and that he would soon realise and want her back, well, she wouldn't wait forever, but she understood he may need to get it out of his system, and she was prepared to let him. She was so sweet and reasonable that Fred almost decided to give Joyce up there and then, but although his head was saying that was the sensible thing to do, he knew his heart was telling him something else.

When the second letter arrived, Fred knew he had made the right choice, her letters were as charming and honest as she was, the idea of her sending him roses made him laugh out loud, and she was so very sweet about how much she cared for him.

Fred told his mother about the roses and showed her the wallet that Joyce had sent him for his birthday, "I think its maybe about time we met your young lady" she said, but it was said with a touch of irony.

Letter Three

68 St Andrews Rd
Cheltenham

18th June 1939

My dear Fred

Thank you for your letter – I've decided to write you a short letter (just by way of being nasty). If you tease me I shall tease you back – that's only fair isn't it? I am supposed to have quite a good sense of humour and I certainly appreciate it in others. This is not a sign for you to get swell headed – not that I think you would. By the way, who put those ideas about telephonists in your head? Actually quite a lot of those in Cheltenham are catty – and they all think a frightful lot of themselves. Of course, I am an exception. The latest craze in the office is 'German' about half a dozen of them have taken it up. I considered it and then I thought that if I decided to swot up on a language it would be French because I already know quite a bit of the groundwork and I was quite good at it when I was young (many years ago)! I told mother I thought of studying German and she just grunted and said "cooking would do you more good".

Still, I'm sure you are not interested in those things, although of course, I could be a German spy or something like that in the case of a war. Still then they would probably shoot me – that would be too tragic wouldn't it? Do you know my dearest, I would tease you to death if you were here, I just feel in the mood.

I'm awfully sorry about your gale yesterday, it was thundery here today but not at all bad yesterday. I absolutely refuse to spoil you further by saying that I excuse your letter (actually I rather liked it)! Although you have written better ones. I had to wait until tea time to read it – I was awfully impatient.

You know it does me good to have you (sounds rather as if I own you doesn't it) because I just have to put up with seeing you once in a blue moon – this is very good for my patience. I am frightfully glad to hear about your 'reforming' Fred dear, you know it makes me the more fond of you to realise that you are doing it because I asked you. It sounds as if I have got a good opinion of myself but I don't really mean it that way. It's for your own good dearest – I've come to the conclusion I ought to have been a preacher. Don't you think I would have made a good one?

By the way, I mustn't have such long phone calls to you in the future, not more that a quarter of an hour at the most! It's better, because then nobody will notice them. Somehow you seem further away than you have for a long time, I don't like feeling that it is so, I want you to write to me and tell me that you think of me an awful lot. You do don't you? The worst of it is being so far away, I don't have the chance to influence you at all. I mean I have to risk the fact that you may get fed up writing to me – of course I don't think you will, but it is a possibility. I hate to write to you like this but somehow I just can't help thinking that I'd be frightfully hurt if anything like that did happen. Please forgive me for being so morbid dear.

It was rotten luck that you were prevented from coming to see me on Sunday, I was disappointed but I realise that it couldn't be helped. Somehow fate is trying his hardest, but we won't be beaten will we? I think I shall just about survive until I see you again.

Must close now Fred dear.

Your own

Joyce

P.S.

Of course you will write as soon as possible won't you?

Goodnight dearest.

The next letter arrived mid morning and dropped onto the hall rug with an ominous plop. It was rare for Fred to be at home on a Friday, but he had a few days holiday to use up. He was a little reluctant to open this one, he knew that Joyce was annoyed with him, or at least she had been when he'd spoken to her on Sunday. It had been a very lengthy phone call, he had had to tell her on Saturday that he was unable to make it to Cheltenham and she had been extremely disappointed and not entirely convinced by the apologies and regrets on his side. She had said it was quite beyond the pale that the coach company had cancelled the service at the last minute, and it was a disgrace that they had given such short notice, and where would we be if everyone cancelled everything whenever they felt like it? He had let her have her say but actually had found it rather amusing and had teased her dreadfully which had not helped her mood at all.

It was quite a short letter by Joyce's standards but then his letter to her hadn't been very long either. His friends had been ribbing him he had said, about the glamorous young telephonist that he was stepping out with, so you see, he had said, he was being teased too, he had thought this would make her smile and undo some of the damage caused by his absence on Sunday. Judging from her letter she was only slightly mollified. He told her about the awful weather they had been having in the Midlands, it had been really quite cold and wintery for the time of year and there had been a real gale on the Wednesday. When he'd read the letter over, he'd decided that it was a bit dull and not at all entertaining so he had told her that he intended to become a reformed character as she had requested, and not go out every night, drink and smoke (a little) less, and to think of her every day without fail, that was the easy part, he thought ruefully.

Given that they had only known each other for a few weeks their romance seemed to be one of infinite possibilities. Fred had grown extremely fond of Joyce and it was clear from her correspondence that she was more than a little in love with him; he wondered where it would go and if they really had a chance of a future together. His mother was naturally cautious about the relationship, but not judgemental, and his friends seemed to find the whole situation somewhat amusing.

Normally Fred considered himself to be a very level headed person but meeting Joyce had thrown him sideways and no mistake, he was still trying to digest everything that had happened. He must try and get to see her soon, he thought, it was a lot easier to envisage a future together when they were actually with each other.

In his more thought provoking moments Fred did wonder if it was wise to be pursuing any sort of relationship at all, although the talk of war was not always taken seriously it had to be acknowledged as a real possibility. What would he do if it did become reality? He would have to fight, it was a question of whether he joined up or waited to be called up. His mother was, not too surprisingly, reluctant to discuss it at all, and when all was said and done, he was the man of the house since his father had left home, swiftly followed by his much older brother and he felt her apprehensiveness keenly. It was a funny old world, never knowing from one day to the next what fate had in store for you, he wished he could be back in Skegness again, where they had been so carefree and had such a jolly time. He wondered when, and if, they would ever have days like that again. God, why couldn't folk just learn to live in peace together, surely there was enough world to go round, it was a big enough place for goodness sake.

Fred was starting to feel morbid now so he reread Joyce's letter. He was really quite astonished that she seemed to care for him so much, and more importantly, wasn't afraid to tell him. It made a refreshing change as, in his experience, a lot of the girls he had met previously seemed to be quite buttoned up when it came to expressing their feelings and had seemed more interested in playing silly games. Joyce was different, maybe it was a confidence thing, or perhaps it was simply that she hadn't learnt the art of deception, that her world was more black and white, because she hadn't been hurt yet she didn't know how to be clever or contrived, she could only be honest and it made all her all the more delightful and agreeable, He would have to be very careful not to hurt her, intentionally or otherwise. Gosh, he really was becoming a reformed character.

He wondered what Joyce's parents thought of him, he had only met her mother briefly, and her father he was yet to be introduced to. Did they approve? Would he be deemed suitable husband material? Goodness he did have it bad, husband material is it now? Reading the letter again he had thought it odd that some of Joyce's colleagues were considering learning German, given the state of unrest at the moment, he imagined that they were probably jesting or at least not being completely honest, he thought French a much better option and would tell her so. He decided to write her a really long letter to make up for the last one, he would try to write a really splendid 'epistle' – one that would make her smile and love him all the more.

He started writing, Dear Joyce How are you!

Letter Four

68 St Andrews Rd
Cheltenham

23rd June 1939

Getting near bedtime

Dearest Fred

Thank you so much for your lengthy epistle. It was nice to get a really long letter – I shall know what to do next time I require one! Of course I looked for a letter on Wednesday, but somehow didn't think you would manage it – still your letters are worth waiting for so I'll forgive you (very sweet natured what?) I shall have to continue this tomorrow as it's getting quite late. I'm glad you approve of French – I shall probably commence writing to you in 'le francais' when I have done some studying of the language. Le début mon cher Fred, merci beaucoup for votre letter, el est arrivée ce martin, bon soir mon ami, je vous aime beaucoup. Oh dear, I'm afraid I've forgotten every bit of grammar I ever knew, terrible, n'est-ce pas? So until I consider myself to be a capable French correspondent I shall have to stick to our own humble language.

You know, your letter was too nice for me to try and answer. Of course, I don't believe you could be brutal to me if you tried, I should probably get vicious and bite or kick, or maybe both, how would you like that! I am teasing you again aren't I? You asked me if I could recall where those photos were taken at Skegness, do you think I am likely to forget? I agree with you that we were happy, but then, whenever people are happy, something has to happen to spoil that happiness, it seems to be one of the laws of life! I mean, it would have been impossible for us to stay at Skegness for long together wouldn't it? After all, I have still got you now, and you have got me – just because I'm a long way away, it doesn't alter my feelings – if it did then they wouldn't be worth worrying about would they? You know *dear, I don't like your attitude about me "liking you' I see nothing unusual in it myself, and as for me being too nice for you – its absolute rubbish, and I absolutely <u>forbid</u> you to bring the subject up again – when you write to me like that it makes me feel that you are a little boy who someone has hurt, and I want to take you in my arms and comfort you. I should make an enormous fuss of you and I should expect you to make a fuss of me as well. Fred dear I certainly must go to bed now, I do love to think of you feeling like that about me when you go to bed – I promise you that you will be the last thing in my thoughts tonight. Goodnight Fred.*

Hello dear, it's Friday now, what a day! I worked until eight this evening and I feel rather worn out – also in a filthy temper because the person who was supposed to be supervising us this evening had a minor row with me, She told me I had no right to think! All I had to do, was to do as I was told! Anyhow, she is not in a position to boss me about with that kind of talk, and it made me really cross. Sorry dearest, but I felt really sore about it, as you can see, I can get most annoyed when people cross me (this is a warning) Still, I'm sure you wouldn't try to cross me too much would you? Anyway, I shouldn't mind you ordering me around, it would be completely different! I'm afraid this letter wont be frightfully long because I must catch the last post with it, else I should have you wondering what has become of me. Being conceited, I know it would worry you if you don't receive this on Saturday morning. Fred dear, I'll ring you at the usual place at 11.45 am if that's ok ? If I don't ring immediately please wait, I promise you I'll be there – also dear, a gentle hint, don't go and play bowls at Spencer park at the last minute and forget all about me (you couldn't could you?) And then arrive, out of breath and too flustered to talk to me – else I shall manage to ring you up about a quarter of an hour late. You know, I'm getting quite good at teasing you, don't you agree?

By the way, I had a brainwave this morning. Of course its up to you Fred dear, but it's August bank holiday in a few weeks time and I thought that maybe you could come for the whole weekend, you know I'd love to have you to visit – but as I said before, its up to you. I haven't spoken to you on the phone for simply ages, I'm so looking forward to Sunday and hearing your voice, I know you will say 'how are you?'

I hope your friend Tommy or do you prefer Tom? I notice that you call him either, anyway I hope you have successfully fixed your wedding (his wedding!)

I assure you Fred dear, I enjoyed reading your letter, I enjoy reading all your letters. Somehow part of you belongs in the letters you write to me. Although, letters are said to express thoughts badly, I disagree, they help convey a feeling of nearness which somewhat bridges the gap of a hundred or so miles. Still, what are a few miles to people like us, Un bagatelle!

Dearest Fred, I really must go now, I hope to hear from you on Sunday and of course I'm hoping to see you soon.

So until Sunday my dearest, Goodnight Fred

Your own

Joyce

Fred opened the fourth letter without a moment's hesitation, he really looked forward to reading them now, they always managed to brighten his day. He had made a particular effort with his last correspondence and was pleased that Joyce was so delighted with it. He thought her attempts at French were really quite comical, although he would not have been able to do any better himself, he was sure. In actual fact he thought she had done very well and was quietly impressed. He was glad that she remembered Skegness with so much affection, if only they could visit again. It would have been splendid if they could have spent the weekend of the August holiday there but he guessed this would be impossible so he put his mind to thinking of alternative arrangements.

He thought that it would be a lot simpler if he were to visit Joyce and not visa versa, although his mother was very keen to meet her, he wasn't sure how Joyce's parents would feel about her travelling alone to Coventry and staying with a man, who, in their eyes, she hardly knew, albeit with a constant chaperone. Fred had spoken to his mother on the subject, and she agreed that, whilst Joyce would be very welcome and could be easily accommodated, it would be far more sensible for Fred to go to Cheltenham. It would give Joyce's parents a chance to get to know him better she had said and maybe if they saw how fond of each other they were, then perhaps they would be happier to let her travel up to stay with Fred by herself.

Fred hadn't played bowls on Sunday so he was by the phone ready to take her call at 11.45 as requested and they chatted away quite happily, discussing everything and nothing and all things in between, that was until Joyce had mentioned the possibility of war. Even the mention of it made Fred feel a little down, actually, a lot down, he decided that they should keep things light and not discuss it, only talk of jolly things, he had said, if that was possible. Joyce seemed remarkably stoic about the prospect of conflict, far more than he was, she seemed to look on it as inevitable and simply accepted the fact, that was part of her innocence, and he couldn't help but like her all the more for it. But it was hard to escape from it, the papers were full of news and speculation, and nobody really seemed to know what was happening in reality. Hitler had invaded Czechoslovakia in March and Britain had begun re-arming, conscription was reintroduced and assurances given to Poland, whatever that meant, who were being threatened by Hitler. Fred had heard plenty of horror stories about World War 1 and he knew that another war would be catastrophic, indeed anyone with a modicum of sense would know that it would be brutal. He thought again of the wisdom of falling in love in such dubious times, If that's what he was doing! But then, he thought, the world would keep on turning on its axis regardless, and however bleak the future, surly it was better to grasp any happiness that you could along the way. After all it may never happen, and besides, if, or rather once Britain was involved, surely it wouldn't last for long, be over before you knew it, at least that's what the talk in the pub was, when he was sat around the table with his drinking pals. They all seemed to treat the possibility off war as a bit of an escapade, something that would bring a bit of excitement into their lives. Some of the lads were already planning on signing up, it was just a question of deciding which branch of the armed forces they fancied. Oh the innocence of it all. Perhaps they were right, perhaps it might never happen anyway.

Fred sat down and decided to write to Joyce with a lighter heart. He hadn't written on Sunday because of his indecision regarding the August bank holiday, but had now quite made up his mind that if Joyce couldn't get her parents to agree to her visiting Coventry, then he would go to Cheltenham. He would travel by coach on the Saturday morning, perhaps, if possible, Friday evening and they could have the whole weekend together as he wouldn't have to leave until Monday evening. He would ask her to think of things they could do together, things that they would both enjoy, and he would be especially nice to her and not tease her so terribly and she would be very sweet and caring and worry and fuss over him. He would be awfully nice to her mother as well, he would be especially charming to her, and very polite and deferential to her father. Of course he hadn't met Mr Wright yet but was sure that it would not be a problem. It suddenly occurred to him, whilst he was thinking about it, that he was actually stepping out with Miss Wright, well, if that wasn't an omen what was?

His mother was a little disappointed that she wasn't going to meet Fred's young lady yet, she suggested that Joyce really must visit him next time, it was important that they got together, as it was important that she could feel that she knew and liked the girl. She trusted Fred's judgement, she knew he wasn't a fickle lad, but nevertheless it was time they all met. She even suggested that she might accompany him to Cheltenham, perhaps book into a small guest house for a couple of evenings but Fred said it would be better if he got to know her parents a little better first and she reluctantly concurred. In actual fact it would be quite nice to have the place to herself for the weekend, sharing her home with a love-struck young man could be rather tiring she thought.

Letter Five

68 St Andrews Rd
Cheltenham

Friday 14th July

My dearest Fred

Thank you so much for your letter – I'm awfully sorry that you didn't feel like writing to me on Sunday afternoon – you know it isn't good for you to feel morbid. Actually I felt as you did later, that compared to some unfortunate people we have very little to feel morbid about. It's a great deal better to count one's blessings than to bemoan one's fate, which can't be altered anyway! Don't you agree? To continue, thanks for the press cutting, I really enjoyed reading it and I like to have things like that, that interest you, because therefore they are of interest to me also.

By the way, as far as I can see, I don't seem to be able to get a half day on August Saturday but I haven't given up trying. Still Fred dear, I don't mind so very much, as long as we are together for the weekend. Of course I should loved to have come to Coventry and see your home and your people, and meet some of your friends again, but I guess it will have to wait until another time. At least we will be together which is all I can ask.

That reminds me dear, I was talking quite casually to my mother about the visit etc and I gathered from what she said that I would not be allowed to go any old place with you. If I stayed at your home, that would be permissible, but otherwise, she says, it just isn't done. Why not? I don't personally see why. I hope you don't mind me writing to you about this, but I thought I perhaps ought to let you know how things are – I know you will understand – although I'm beggared if I do, anyhow, we can talk it over when we are together.

I don't know why it is, but parents always seem to have different ideas on various subjects from their children, which they then try to enforce on the latter! They say, when you are older you will understand and realise it is for the best – I sometimes wonder! Actually I believe my parents aren't in any position to take such a narrow attitude towards life. I wish I was of age like you and then I could just do as I liked – I'm quite sure that I would have enough common sense to do the right things. You will be thinking that I'm getting morbid next if I continue in this vein so I'll change the subject.

How's your work going? I haven't heard you mention having to work late just recently. I must confess I'm rather fed up with it, my work I mean, I've been working until eight o'clock on overtime the last two evenings and I am really rather irritated with it. Still, I could do with the money so I have no need for grumbling. I was going swimming yesterday but it was so beastly cold that I decided I wouldn't, It's lovely having an outdoor pool but I must admit it can be rather bracing, I had no-one to drag me in by brute force as you did in Skegness. You know I had absolutely made up my mind that you would enter the water that day – I suppose it was a case of mind over matter (may I tease you?)

I must close soon or I shan't get this to the post, by the way, I hope that you will excuse the paper, its Elsie's typing paper (I had run out). I rather like it to write on. Elsie has gone to the pictures with a boyfriend for the first time, shan't we tease her when she returns home. He seems like an awful little infant to me, I suppose, like you, I must be getting old, although I haven't discovered a white hair!

I have been thinking (unusual for me I admit) touching on your forbidden subject – if you feel like that about things in general, I wonder what motive prompted you to continue a correspondence and also visit, a girl whom you met, quite accidentally, for only a few days, whilst you were on holiday. It would have been very easy to drop the whole thing (how glad I am that you didn't Fred dear) but I think it should prove to you that you are a lot nicer than you seem to think you are, you really are frightfully nice sometimes – I suppose you have to be in the right mood, and at other times you tease me mercilessly, but I guess I can put up with your teasing as long as you are nice to me as well. I really must close now, I shall have to run to post this. Goodnight Fred dearest.

Your very own

Joyce

P.S.

Of course I liked your ten page epistle, this isn't exactly a hint, but please please write soon.

P.P.S.

I should also love you to kiss me goodnight — but I shall have to imagine it – anyhow, I shall see you soon.

Fred's mother set down a cup of tea by his side and placed the letter next to it, "another one for you love" she smiled. He had smiled back, relaxed back in his armchair and opened the letter. As was his way, he read it through once quickly, barely skimming the words, and then re read it at a more leisurely pace. Joyce's conversation with her mother as regards to them not being able to go (any old place together) seemed to him to be very sensible, he could quite see that it would not be deemed proper for them to go anywhere unchaperoned, in fact, he thought that Joyce was being rather unreasonable in her protestations, and it struck him that Joyce could be a little headstrong at times, which alarmed him a little but also made him smile. And what did she mean when she said that she didn't think her parents were in a position to take such a narrow attitude on life. Was there a hint of scandal in the household? Very intriguing.

He was really quite pleased about going to see Joyce, and getting to know her and her family better. It would be good to get out of Coventry for the weekend, not that Cheltenham was a particularly exciting place to visit, actually, thought Fred, that was a bit unfair, as he hadn't really seen much of the actual town but it would make a nice change and he was looking forward to spending time with Joyce. Hopefully they would be able to spend some time alone with each other, although he knew that there would be plans with the family as well.

He was glad that she had enjoyed reading the article he had sent her, it was a piece about Amelia Earhart, who, of course, had disappeared two years earlier, along with her navigator, whilst trying to circumnavigate the globe. He had particularly liked Amelia Earhart's reply when she was asked, regarding her solo flight across the Atlantic ocean, "Why do it?" She answered thus, "Have you ever longed to go to the North pole? Or smell overripe apples in the sunshine? Or coast down a steep snow covered hill to an unknown valley? Or take a job behind a counter selling ribbons and show people how to sell ribbons as ribbons have never been sold before? Or take a friend by the arm and say 'Forget it – I'm with you forever' Or just before a thunderstorm, to turn ten somersaults on the lawn?" Fred thought it was an excellent answer, and he guessed that Joyce would like it too, she was an incurable romantic and would love the idea of turning ten somersaults on the lawn, he could almost picture her now.

When he had read the letter through again he placed it on the small table by the side of the chair and gave some thought to the last few lines that Joyce had written. She had made a valid point, he'd wondered himself about the common sense aspect of getting into a new relationship at this particular time in his life, perhaps he hadn't really thought that it would go anywhere. It was, as Joyce had said, she was a girl he had met quite accidentally for a few days whilst on holiday by the seaside, he didn't need to see her again, he had still got good old dependable Irene waiting here in Coventry for him, he could have simply have kissed her goodbye and left it at that, and dropped the whole thing. Why didn't he, Joyce said that she was awfully glad that he hadn't, and now, after some initial doubts, he was awfully glad too. Ah well, the path of true love etc etc, but it was still going to be complicated.

Fred had had a long overdue chat with his mother the previous evening, he thought it only fair to let her know about his long term plans, good lord, that made it sound very formal. He wanted to get to know Joyce a lot better, but generally speaking he felt that he could see a future for them both. Of course, he would expect Joyce to move to Coventry and they would have to live with his mother for at least a couple of years, Fred hadn't been very ambitious up to now but he had the sense to realise that he would have to work a lot harder if there was to be any chance of promotion and he had already started to volunteer for any overtime going. His mother had seemed quite amenable to the suggestions, but it was easy when she didn't really think it would happen. The house was big enough, she had said, but how would Joyce feel about leaving her family? Fred had not really considered this, she was obviously very close to her mother, the father, he wasn't so sure about. Would she want to up sticks and leave her job and her friends to move to a strange city with a man, that despite her protestations, she hardly knew.

Fred sighed, it was no good speculating, nothing would be decided for a long time, and besides, if, or rather when, war came it would change everything anyway, he would almost certainly have to join up, and he could end up who knows where. Still, at least they would have the weekend, they must make the most of it and put the future on the back burner for now, life would take over soon enough and choices would be made for them, no doubt, whether they liked them or not. So, the upshot of his musings took Fred back, very firmly, to square one, he decided that no decisions should be made today, or indeed in the near future, he would simply enjoy himself at the weekend and wait to see what would happen over the next few months.

Frightfully good idea, time for a pint.

Letter Six

68 St Andrews Rd
Cheltenham

Thursday 3rd August

Dear Fred

Thanks so much for your letter – I knew you would write on Tuesday. I'm all by myself this evening. I'm looking after Mrs Collins whilst mother goes out with a friend. I can't write to you for an awful long time because I have to wash my hair – a very lengthy job – as I've got rather a lot. I didn't like your remark about the swimming pool! Anyhow just to be annoying I had two friends from the office for tea and we all went swimming, temp 64 degrees, it was a trifle cold.

Mrs Collins and I get on beautifully together, it's quite a relief to be able to do things in perfect quiet without numerous noisy interruptions. On Tuesday we had a boy, I guess you would call him a lad, he's nineteen, to tea, he's something in the airforce, also an orphan, and stays when on leave, with his sister in Cheltenham. Mother generally mothers him up and fusses over him, as is her way, and he always visits us when around. The strange thing about it is that his home was in Coventry – I never really liked him, but realising he came from there I made myself as agreeable as possible as somehow it made me feel closer to you.

You asked me to think of something for us to do over the weekend. You know by now that I consider that you should decide the things that should be done – however I'll try and think and as I want to talk to you on the subject I shall endeavour to ring you up at the office between five and six tomorrow (Friday) If I don't manage it you'll know something unforeseen has occurred. We've had a frightful day at work

31

today – an exchange which we work for went out of order – only one line remained – every call had to be logged and put through in rotation in the order of booking – it was pretty impossible and I was unfortunate enough to have to deal with it part of the morning.

Two of my friends have just arrived and they have commenced to chatter and talk to me. I implored them to shut up while I wrote to you – but it seems to have no effect on them. They are a frightful noisy lot so I guess I shall have to finish this and amuse them. I am sorry that this is such a short and miserable epistle dear but if only you knew what I have to contend with! Its time for me to see to the supper now. I really must close now dear, you know I'll be thinking of you don't you? It will be heavenly to have you here for the weekend – so until Saturday – goodnight.

Hope to speak to you tomorrow.

Your own

Joyce

The sixth letter was short and sweet and very Joyce, she really was very mercurial, Fred chuckled to himself as he read it, he hadn't got a clue who Mrs Collins was, an elderly neighbour perhaps, who needed looking after, invited round for tea and sympathy. He could just imagine Joyce now, fussing over her and making sure she was comfortable, laying the table and clattering the teacups, the best china perhaps? Maybe they would get the best china out for him as well when he was there.

Fred was catching the coach to Cheltenham the following day and would be staying for the whole weekend. Although his mind was pretty much made up as regards to his future with Joyce he had decided to try and keep it as casual as possible. The talk of war was still on everyone's lips, without a doubt, it was now inevitable and he was very conscious of the unfairness of declaring undying love to her when they might never have the chance of a future together. He realised that couples all over the country must be having the same misgivings and deciding to follow their hearts regardless but he was determined to try and keep it relaxed if he could, he wondered if he would still be able to feel such resolve when he was holding Joyce in his arms under the moonlight, whilst she gazed up at him quietly humming under her breath in a way that she had, that he found simply enchanting.

He also thought it quite amusing that she considered him to be in charge of their activities, Joyce had clearly decided that he was the man of the house already! Fred wondered how long that would last. He also wondered what it was that she had been thinking about and what the particular subject was that she wanted to talk to him about. She hadn't really had much time to chat when she had phoned him earlier, work had been manic and working overtime had been expected for the whole exchange.

He wondered who the 'lad' was that she had mentioned and why, he thought, she hadn't mentioned him before, she hadn't even told him his name, only that he was also from Coventry, Fred might even know him, it was extremely unlikely but possible. He had to confess to himself that he felt a little jealous, he wasn't sure he liked the idea of his girl entertaining a nineteen year old to tea, something in the airforce indeed!!!

He started to worry that perhaps Joyce had also come to realise that they really shouldn't be thinking long term as regards to their relationship. Although she was young, and in many ways extremely innocent there was also a very practical and realistic side to her. Moreover Fred got the impression that if she was up against it and the chips were down Joyce could be a very formidable opponent, certainly one that he wouldn't relish crossing. She was however also very traditional and believed that the man should make the important decisions where a relationship was concerned.

There was no doubt that some very important decisions were going to have to be made and soon, Fred had decided that if he was going to have to join up it would be the Navy. Although he had tried to bring this up with his mother it was a subject that she frowned upon. She had chosen to believe that, even if war was declared it would be over in a matter of months and unless Fred actually volunteered he may never need to fight. She had up till now refused point blank to talk about it with him; but it would have to be talked about and talked about soon. Fred didn't consider himself to be a particularly heroic man but he had guts and knew what his duty was to King and Country. What was the quote he had read recently, "True courage is in facing danger even when you are afraid", sometimes Fred felt very afraid. Thank goodness for the bank holiday weekend, two days away, glorious weather forecast and a beautiful young lass on his arm gazing up at him with unconditional devotion. Heaven!

Letter Seven

68 St Andrews Rd
Cheltenham

Wednesday 9th August

Dearest Fred

I hope you got back home safely yesterday. I did think that perhaps you would drop me a few lines to say you'd arrived back ok, but I guess you must have been too busy one way or another. I have missed you, I had just got used to having you around and then off you have to go. Now everything seems so frightfully uninteresting and quiet. I suppose you must have a magnetic personality which makes your absence felt. I trust that you haven't developed a cold yet? I think it would serve you right if you did – I should absolutely refuse to be sympathetic. Actually I'm feeling very annoyed.

Item 1 for annoyance

We've had air raid warning practise during the day.

Item 2

I arrived home to find the front door locked and I had to get through the kitchen window, a difficult and very unladylike achievement I'm afraid. It's a good job I'm so slim and supple don't you think!

Item 3

Also, my tea was left on a tray and mother had gone out to a W.I. meeting with cousin Isabelle

Do you think I had cause to be annoyed dear? Of course I was still feeling sore about your departure, I'm so glad I was able to see you off after all – I can't tell you how miserable I felt at dinner time when you left me at the exchange – I just couldn't have said any more to you because I was feeling pretty awful. Anyhow, to look on the best side of it – it was marvellous to have you for the whole weekend dear, the only thing I don't like about it is, that every time I see you I become more fond of you – and consequently hate you having to go – but this is rather stupid because I know you don't like leaving either and it makes it all the better the next time we meet.

I have had time to realise and respect your good qualities (I grant you they are few and far between) may I tease you? I'm afraid I can't write you for much longer as I have to go out. It seems awful to have to write to you when only yesterday you were here to talk to and live with. Mother seems to have fallen for you, I'm frightfully jealous – because I am a very selfish person and want you all for myself.

How's the work going dear? Not too well I guess. About Sunday dear, I'm working 9.30 - 1.30 so shall I ring you up some time before, or after? Preferably after I think, knowing how long it takes you to arise in the morning! Anyhow perhaps you'd let me know what time would suit you and I'll endeavour to fit in with your requirements. I really am an awfully obliging person aren't I? If the time isn't suitable I'll let you know so don't delay writing to me for too long – or else nothing will be arranged – I'm just going to a concert with some females from the office, I'd rather be going out with you.

I definitely prefer male company to female (sorry) providing it's the right person. It would be just perfect for you to hold me for just one minute, then I would feel quiet happy, it's funny how happy I do feel when I'm with you, I do hope you feel the same way dear – I think you do – I really have to go now although I don't want to. Please write to me soon dear, if it can't be a long letter I'll understand you're busy.

Goodnight, Fred dearest.

Your very own

Joyce

Fred read the seventh letter with a tinge of guilt, he had been remiss in not jotting down a few lines to let Joyce know that he had arrived home safely, although, he thought, there was no reason to suppose otherwise. They had had a lovely few days together, the weather, for a change had been perfect, those long, glorious summer days and beautiful warm evenings, days that reminded him of his childhood, carefree and innocent with the future bright and inviting and everything to look forward to. He felt that he and Joyce had grown much closer over the weekend, they had talked about the war, no one pretended that it was only a possibility anymore, the consensus was that it was inevitable. Generally everyone went about their lives as usual, working round various disruptions, like Joyce's annoying air raid practise! But there was also a look of fear in the eyes of the ordinary people on the streets and the cafes and in the cinema queues. Storm clouds where gathering and the world was beginning to look like a much darker place.

Although Joyce was eternally optimistic, Fred also knew that deep down she was as fearful about the prospect of war as he and everyone else was. They both no longer felt (had Joyce ever felt?) that it was unwise to carry on a relationship that may have no future, rather, their feelings were that they must grab at any chance of happiness whilst they could, and without being too foolish they had made the most of every moment over their precious few days together.

It had been quite a wrench when they had parted, originally they had had to say goodbye at the exchange as Joyce was supposed to be working and it was agreed that he would stop by on his way to the bus station. Joyce's supervisor was unwilling to allow her to accompany Fred to the terminus but when he had said goodbye to her at the exchange she had been so distraught he was reluctant to leave. Joyce's supervisor, realising her distress when he'd gone had let her go after him and they managed a fond and passionate farewell just before he had to board his coach. In truth, they were both miserable at the parting, it was getting harder and harder for them to say goodbye.

That evening Fred and his mother had a long and involved chat about the situation, but there really wasn't anything to discuss, Fred felt in his heart that Joyce was the one for him. Had he known all along, right from that first day on the seafront at Skegness, possibly, the question now was, said his mother, did Joyce feel he same? Fred had no doubts at all on that score, he was as sure of her feelings as he could possibly be, his question was, did they hold back and wait to see what would happen over the coming months or did he take the plunge and ask for her hand, or rather ask her father as she was not of age yet and they would need her parents' permission. To be honest, thought Fred ruefully, there was no guarantee at all that they would give it.

Letter Eight

68 St Andrews Rd
Cheltenham

11th August 1939

Dearest Fred

Thanks for your letter, I received it today, I'm writing you a few lines to suggest I ring you at 3pm on Sunday – I seem to remember that your dinner time on Sunday is 1.30pm; I would hate to be the cause of you being late for dinner – perhaps you will make an effort and be on time will you? – and I'll ring you at 3pm, I shall ring you from the Woodhouse exchange, I'm going to be there all day (It's only a country place) so that the people who work there can go to the sea for the day. The girl is a friend of mine at work, she was going to make a four if Bob had come down that time, remember? I shall have very little to do in the afternoon but if I'm a little late ringing you'll understand and wait won't you dear?

Sorry you had a rotten journey, I thought about you.

It's been a marvellous day today, I went to tea with my grandmother and visited my cousin Mark and he explained the workings of their new car, I have hopes of him teaching me to drive (when he's passed his own test) then I can steal or borrow a car and visit you.

This evening I have been playing tennis, the first time in weeks – I must be getting frightfully chubby, my shorts hardly seem to meet round me – terrible isn't it. I'm sorry your letter was so short but it was very nice, and of course I understand.

Can't stop now dear, this is only to let you know for Sunday - I'm in a frightful hurry, witness the handwriting!

Your own

Joyce

P.S. I hope your mother feels better

It had been an absolutely awful journey back from Cheltenham, the weather had taken a turn for the worst and the coach had been damp and crowded, why would so many people want to travel to Coventry? There had been an accident on the main road just the other side of Evesham and they were stuck on the coach for almost two hours, all Fred had with him was a bag of lemon sherbets which he felt obliged to share with his fellow passengers. Actually the atmosphere on the coach became quite jolly, somebody even started a singsong, good old fashioned ditties like *Daisy Daisy* and *Old MacDonald had a farm* with everyone going full pelt on the E.I.E.I.O bits, it got a bit sombre when *Pack up your troubles* started at the rear of the bus followed by *I wonder who's kissing her now* and the passengers became a little melancholy. Of course the accident meant that Fred was late arriving back home and he was concerned that his mother would be worried. As it happened his mother had not been feeling too chipper and had gone to bed before he got home leaving a note and a ham sandwich, curling at the sides (the ham sandwich, not the note) in the fridge for him. It didn't look terribly appetising but he ate it nonetheless – lemon sherbets were not very filling.

The next morning Fred's mother, although a little brighter, still felt under the weather and decided to spend the morning with her feet up and so Fred fussed around looking after her and helping with the household chores. He did wonder if it was simply a case of her feeling a little sad and sorry for herself, he knew that she was worried about the war, the probability of which grew ever more likely. Also she was concerned for her son and his future on more than one level, on so many levels in fact. Fred was at a loss as to how he could help, he felt her distress keenly as he was a sensitive young man, but he was also practical, there would be a war, of that he was now sure, it would take a miracle to avoid conflict now, and, God willing, he would marry Joyce, at least he hoped he would, might help if he asked her first he thought to himself, the question was, when...

Her latest letter had been very short, in fact she really hadn't said much at all, just about phoning him on Sunday, although she had asked after his mother. Her letters didn't seemed as focused on the two of them as they had been, or perhaps he was reading too much into them, starting to feel he was losing the upper hand maybe, if indeed he had ever had it!! She seemed to be so busy these days, work took up a lot of time obviously, plenty of overtime to be had at the moment, but she also seemed to be going out a lot more. It seemed to Fred that the closer he got to her the further away she appeared to be. He decided that he would write Joyce a really long letter, explaining his feeling, how much he cared for her and how he worried that they could sustain their relationship over such a long distance and in such difficult times. He wondered how Joyce really felt about him and he needed to know why she appeared to adore him so much. Was it simply a holiday romance, bringing some much needed excitement into a young girl's, lets face it, rather mundane life, or was it much more than that? He had certainly never felt this way before, not with any of his other, to use an old fashioned term, sweethearts, but was he simply responding to the fear that he felt about the future, was he not just being a little gung-ho about the whole situation, throwing caution to the wind, all that eat, drink and be merry stuff, for tomorrow we may die! God, he was getting morbid again, time to put the kettle on he thought and went through to the parlour to see how his mother was feeling.

41

They sat and drank their tea together and talked quietly about the future and what it might hold. Fred's mother confessed her fears and Fred confessed his, and sad to say a few tears were shed. In the end though, they both felt better and more prepared for what was to come, no-one really knows what the future holds, Fred's mother said, we must be strong and follow our hearts come what may.

Letter Nine

68 St Andrews Rd
Cheltenham

15th August 1939

Dearest Fred

Thank you so much for your letter, I'm glad it was such a nice one. I was at work today so I had to wait until dinner time for my eagerly awaited epistle – it's funny what a difference a letter from you can make – all morning I seemed to think – I shall have a letter from Fred at dinner time, and now I have it beside me. I thought that we had a pretty good 'phone call' don't you? You said a lot of nice things to me, which you don't usually rise to, but I guess you think, at least I hope you do.

How I wish I could go for a walk with you and watch the stars come out, it would be perfect – you say you wonder how I can get pleasure out of just walking with you, I should think that you should realise by now that I get pleasure out of doing anything with you. I could just do absolutely nothing in your company and be perfectly happy, it's funny isn't it? By the way, I don't like the way you rub in the fact that I said "I didn't know why I was so fond of you". The fact remains that I am frightfully fond of you, you know that dear. I will now endeavour to sort out and convey to you the reason for my affection for you.

Firstly. I was attracted by your friendly and jolly appearance on first acquaintance.

Secondly. I realised that you were, in reality, quite a serious person, with a rather disillusioned attitude towards life and people. Obviously you had been treated badly by fate – naturally I felt sympathetic towards you – I felt you needed my love and trust, which I endeavoured to give to you. All this

43

happened at Skegness, afterwards you were so sweet, thoughtful and kind to me that how can I do other than be very fond of you.

You know it's difficult to explain when you are so far away, but you do understand don't you Fred dear? Do you think that I have sufficiently proved to you that I do care for you more than just a little bit? If not I will have to do so next time I see you.

I agree with your ideas on jealousy absolutely, after all, trust is the proof of affection don't you agree? Still, it's frightfully easy to be jealous when you're fond of a person. I refuse to be jealous over you because I'm quite sure that there is no need, tell me there isn't won't you dear.

I love the way that you say we will go to Skegness one day together – it would be perfect wouldn't it? I promise you faithfully that I wouldn't play tennis (with males) before breakfast – instead I would fetch you tea (you would have to fetch it some days) then sit on your bed while you washed... Good idea don't you think? I honestly think you would treat me very well.

I'm afraid this letter won't get posted tonight as the last post has already gone, I played tennis until quite late as I shan't get a chance the rest of the week. Mother is going away tomorrow and 'Aunt Rose' is taking charge of our household. It will be quite ok if you can come on Sunday, I hope you will be able to as it seems a long time since I saw you – I shall possess one virtue as a result of knowing you – and it will be patience.

You know its awful to have perfect days like we have been having lately, blue skies, hot sun and a friendly atmosphere, and then to realise that the only person you really want to share it with is miles away. The evenings seem perfect too, with the moon and stars – it takes me back to Skegness, to those evenings on the beach, remember? When I walk home alone I wish I had you beside me. I hope you don't think I am foolish to think of you like this. I often wonder if you think of me as much as I think of you – I wish that you did.

> *I really must go now dear, please write to me soon. Goodnight Fred*
>
>
> *Your very own*
>
> *Joyce*

Fred was ridiculously pleased when Joyce's letter arrived on Thursday morning, he happened to have the morning off as he had a dentist appointment which rather fortunately had been cancelled. This meant that he could sit down, write back to Joyce and get it in the post the same day. He had some bad news for her and wanted to let her know as soon as possible, if he posted the letter before lunchtime she would get it by Friday. He was feeling a bit down in the dumps actually, they had planned that he would visit on Sunday but he had been unable to make the arrangements, it had been entirely his own fault and he was kicking himself that he hadn't requested the Monday off from work in time.

Joyce's letter was very 'Joyce'. Full of affection, philosophy and total nonsense in equal measures. He loved the way she wrote, it was so natural, no airs and graces, just honest and warm. He had to agree with her about a lot of things, especially when she talked about Skegness or the wonderful weather they were experiencing at the moment, gloriously sunny days and soft balmy nights, just perfect for walking with your girl on your arm and taking the air.

Fred knew how disappointed Joyce would be about the weekend, he was disappointed as well, but with one thing and another, it really, in the grand scheme of things, wasn't the most important item on the agenda. He would definitely try and sort something out soon though.

He did wonder sometimes if they would ever see each other again, the threat of war loomed great like a thick black mist, the spectre of which covered the country with gloom and despondency. Although most people he spoke to seemed optimistic and that the outcome was never in doubt, it would all be over in a flash with Germany cowed and broken and Britain triumphant and undefeated. Fred, however, was intelligent enough to know that there would be a terrible price to pay before peace and common sense reigned. A lot of his friends had already decided to join up, Bob and Tom had joined the Army and were already preparing to leave for training camp, they would be sorely missed, especially by the darts team, Bob being the best left handed darts player in Coventry by a mile. Harry had applied to join the RAF. Fred was interested in joining the Marines, he had the physical attributes for it certainly, and he was a jolly good swimmer, as if that was part of the criteria!

He realised after he had finished his letter and read it through that it was a little gloomy, he hadn't meant to sound so despondent, he was going to rewrite it but wanted to get it in the post as soon as possible so decided to send it as it was. Also, he might have a bit more bad news and wanted to be sure before he disappointed her. His mother had thrown, what she would have called, a spanner into the works, concerning the holiday, and he really wasn't sure how to break it to her, he hoped Joyce would understand, she always understood thought Fred, hopefully...

Letter Ten

68 St Andrews Rd
Cheltenham

18th August 1939

Dearest Fred

Thanks for your letter, I'm afraid you sound rather pessimistic about things in general. Of course I'm sorry you can't come on Sunday because you know how I look forward to any opportunity of seeing you. But nevertheless I refuse to think that it is fate being unkind and after all, I'll be seeing you soon. By the way, you didn't mention anything about our holiday, I hope nothing has happened to upset that. Cheer up dearest, I'll be talking to you on Sunday, will 11 o'clock be ok?

I've had a rotten week, mother's away and aunt Rose is pretty hopeless, I could manage a lot better myself – actually she leaves plenty for me to do, I have to come home at 8pm and find Mrs Collins waiting for her supper! Aunt Rose is out so I, of course, have to obligingly get it! Also I had to do some ironing because it wasn't done, I shall be glad when mother comes home. (finis the grumbling, it's nice to get it off my chest.)

I'm going to be relieving at Gloucester for the day tomorrow, I'm getting quite a person of importance in the exchange. I'm frightfully sorry about the letter, I posted it on Wednesday morning for you, sorry Tuesday, I'm tired and don't know what I do mean!! You should have got it Wednesday morning.

Dearest, I must post this now – hope you don't have to work too hard, please find time to think of me won't you, I could do with a spot of cheering up myself, from you of course, I feel quite lonely and neglected.

Must go dearest.

Your very own

Joyce

P.S.

I prefer your other writing paper!

P.P.S.

11 o'clock on Sunday dearest – don't stop being fond of me will you? I just couldn't bear it.

Your Joyce.

The tenth letter arrived by the early post and Fred had plenty of time before he had to leave for work, he sat in the kitchen with a second cup of tea and read the letter through twice, it wasn't a very long letter. That was unusual in itself, Joyce loved to write him long rambling epistles as she called them, it was also rather gloomy in its content, almost as if life was getting the better of her, but, opined Fred, we couldn't all be happy all of the time, even the cheerful and eternally optimistic Joyce. He was genuinely sorry that he hadn't been able to visit on Sunday, even worse he was going to have to tell her that the little holiday they were hoping for was probably not going to happen, actually it most definitely was not going to happen.

Fred's mother had been most emphatic about it, she pointed out to Fred, with a little more force than she would normally use when speaking to her youngest child, that he couldn't possibly take, what amounted to a teenager, ten years his junior, and only having known her for a few months, away to a guest house for a few days, what on earth was he thinking, even if we are living in more enlightened times, she told him, how on earth did he expect Joyce's parents to agree to it, her father would be apoplectic and rightly so.

Fred knew she was right of course, he didn't really need telling. It had been a lovely idea, and it would have been marvellous to have had Joyce all to himself for a few days, but he had always known that it just couldn't happen.

As an alternative, he had suggested that perhaps Joyce could come and stay with them instead, she would have to stay in the spare room of course, but at least they would have time together and she could finally meet his mother. Unfortunately, his mother wasn't amenable to that idea either, she wanted to meet Joyce, naturally, but it wasn't practical at the moment she said, maybe in a month or so, then we would see.

So poor Fred not only had to write to Joyce and tell her the holiday was off but also that his mother had vetoed a possible visit to Coventry. After initially being very keen on the idea, she had now decided that it was too soon, and she didn't think that Joyce's parents would approve. It wasn't a letter he was looking forward to writing, he knew Joyce would be absolutely devastated, she had really set her heart on them being able to spend time together and goodness only knows when he would be able to visit her in Cheltenham again. He really hoped she hadn't mentioned the planned holiday to her parents yet, he was acutely aware that Joyce's parents were rather wary of their romance, although her mother was much more easy going than her father, who, Fred felt, thought he was a bit of buffoon for getting involved with his daughter in the first place, heaven knows what he would have said about them going away together.

Fred didn't reply straightaway to the letter, he needed a bit of time to think about what he would say. Joyce had seemed quite down and he knew that she would not be happy when he explained the situation. She really could be quite headstrong when she was backed into a corner. He decided to be as truthful as possible in explaining his mother's objections, he really did understand what she meant and hoped that Joyce would too. Also, if they were going to end up spending the rest of their lives together, which he felt was more and more likely, then it was extremely important to him that Joyce and his mother started off, if not strictly friends, at least having a mutual respect, and if that meant conceding to her wishes for the time being, then so be it. He knew in his heart that she was right, and he also knew that Joyce's parents would appreciate the sentiment as well. So it was with quite a heavy sigh that he sat down to write, Dear Joyce... so, how are you .... I'm afraid that I have some disappointing news for you ...

He was able to at least end on a lighter note, he'd made friends with a large labrador which seemed to be lost and had spent quite some time going door to door to try and find the owner. The dog seemed very friendly and really took to him, he found the owner out looking for Dusty, as the dog was called, not far from where he lived at the top of the avenue near Spencer park. It made him feel good to see how happy they were to be reunited, one bright spot in an otherwise gloomy day.

Letter Eleven

68 St Andrews Rd
Cheltenham

20th August 1939

Dearest Fred

I honestly thought that you hadn't written to me – no post at dinner time. So I thought I'd play tennis this evening instead of writing to you as I had intended. Anyway at teatime I received your letter, thank you so much for it, and just before 7pm it commenced to pour with rain and thunder, that cut out our tennis and made it possible for me to write to you. It's funny how things arrange themselves isn't it.

I'm awfully sorry that you feel miserable, I'm afraid I felt pretty bad about it yesterday too. I simply couldn't talk to you as I ought to have done, I unintentionally thought it was your fault, you understand how I mean don't you? That you probably didn't want me to come, and then common sense told me that was ridiculous. You know I have got a frightfully good opinion of myself in some ways. When I didn't get a letter this morning it never entered my head that you really hadn't written, I naturally blamed the post, I know that having told me a thing you're not likely to go back on it, it's nice to have a reliable person like you. Only I wish you were just a bit nearer, I really must try and ring you up this week, I would like to hear your sweet voice again. We were both rather miserable conversationalists on Sunday, weren't we dear? I'd made up my mind defiantly that, whatever happened I'd spend that week's holiday somehow and somewhere even if …. well, never mind. I just won't have that one week taken away from me – after all what's one week that fate should grudge us it.

You have probably gathered that I feel a trifle strongly on the subject, perhaps you'll forgive me for laying the law down like that, but really dear, that's how I feel about it. I do hope dear, you'll get over your morbidness soon because you still have me even if I am a long way away (or perhaps the thought doesn't console you). I do hope your mother will feel differently on the matter, but Fred, if she really feels strongly against me coming for goodness sake don't persuade her against her will. I should certainly hate to feel that I was being forced on her as an unwanted guest. You understand don't you, although I'm young I do have a certain amount of pride. Anyway dear, things are sure to work themselves out for the best and we will have our holiday I'm sure.

Mother is coming home tomorrow and she will want to know what I'm doing on my leave, so dear, do try and let me know as soon as possible won't you ....

I've been reading 'Gone with the Wind' Have you read it? It's a good book but I find it hard to understand the characters as realistic humans. To begin with they cram a frightful amount into one short life, especially the heroine who gets married three times! But she's a well drawn character, all through the book she gets her own way, hurting other people, and then at the end she finds she can't have what she wants. Just as I should like to have you here more sometimes – but it's no use wishing.

I thought the part in your letter about you and the lovely dog was very sweet.

I really must close now dear, I hope you'll have time to write me a nice letter soon, but I understand about you having lots of work to do. One day perhaps I'll be able to come and live nearer to you – it would be perfect wouldn't it? Until then we'll manage I guess, you know it provides me with an awful thrill when I do see you. I really must close now, hoping things will turn out ok.

Your very own

Joyce

P.S.

I believe you've forgotten to tease me lately

They had had a very strained conversation on the phone on Sunday morning, as Fred had predicted, Joyce was not happy, her disappointment was palatable and Fred was at a loss as how to handle it. He had to promise that he would talk to his mother and plead their case again, Joyce was simply determined to spend her week's leave with him, come hell or high water, life was getting a little more difficult than Fred was comfortable with; not for the first he wondered if this long distance relationship was quite the best idea he'd ever had!

As it happened, Fred had had a long chat with his mother that very evening,she had been feeling a bit under the weather lately she said, and had perhaps been too harsh with her decision. Now she had calmed down a little, she realised that she may have been a bit hard on the couple, she hated falling out with Fred and knew that he too was very upset with the situation. She still felt that he had been irresponsible in letting Joyce believe that it would be possible for them to go away together unchaperoned, it was only the 1930s after all, and even the threat of war shouldn't result in folk loosing all sense of priority! However, she also realised that the two of them were extremely serious about their relationship and that it was very probable that they may end up getting married one day. In view of this she had revised her position regarding Joyce coming to Coventry and staying with herself and Fred. It seemed to be the best solution, providing, she said, that Joyce's parents were in agreement and she had written confirmation from them saying as much. So it was arranged that Joyce would spend the following week with them.

Fred was delighted with the outcome of their talk, and extremely grateful, he couldn't wait to let Joyce know, he would write straightaway and share the good news. If he was quick he could catch the last post.

Actually it was a pity he hadn't waited until the morning it would have saved a lot of heartache, once again he would have had to disappoint the poor lass, for when Fred woke the following morning there was none of the usual hustle and bustle coming from downstairs and Fred was alarmed to find his mother in bed and rather unwell, the doctor was called and arrived later that morning to declare that Fred's mother was suffering from a severe case of the flu and would need at least two weeks bedrest, and most of all, peace and quiet, there would be no visitors next week after all.

Fred sat down with a heavy heart and wrote to Joyce with a view to catching the lunchtime post. He could have called her at work but he knew it was frowned upon and he didn't want to get her into trouble as well as letting her down, then he would have to arrange for Sylvia, the next door neighbour to come in and look after his mother whilst he was at work, even though his mother had insisted it wasn't necessary, the doctor said it was!

He posted the letter on his way into work, it was full of apologies and a suggestion that they speak on the phone, as usual, on Sunday.

Letter Twelve

68 St Andrews Rd
Cheltenham

24th August 1939

Dearest Fred

Thanks for your letter - I'm frightfully sorry, but, well neither of us are to blame – I hope your mother will feel better soon. At the rate we are going on there will probably be a war long before September so it won't make a lot of difference. We are frightfully overworked at the office, everyone seems to go mad at the thought of a war and they all ring up everyone they possibly can just to be awkward.

How is the world using you Fred dear? I trust you feel more cheerful. We really must have a talk on Sunday and see what's left for us to do. I'm very sorry, but I didn't write to you last night because I just didn't know what to write. It made me feel that someone or something was trying to take you away from me – and I don't want that to happen, although all you do is tease or worry me.

I can't write you very much more this time, but I promise you I'll write you a nice long letter – that's if you'd like me to – would you? About Sunday, I'll ring you up at 11am – ok?

I have been called for by Rachel so I must go out, sorry it's so short, really must go.

Please write soon

Your very own

Joyce

Well, that was rather short and to the point thought Fred when he had read Joyce's latest letter, very un-Joyce like, and rather cold he felt. He folded it up carefully and placed it back in the envelope, he'd have another look at it later. It was the morning of the 25th of August 1939, and for the unsuspecting people of Coventry, an event was about to happen which would shake them to the very core. Fred had got to his office near to the town centre just before 9am, he was feeling quite down in the dumps, all things considered, it had been a very unsatisfactory couple of weeks. Joyce in all her wisdom, could not see why they had not been allowed to go away together, after all, they were both adults. Actually, in Joyce's case she wasn't yet considered as being an adult, and would have needed her parents consent to marry, let alone go on holiday with a beau, especially as they weren't even engaged, or indeed, had even talked about a possible engagement as yet. Although Joyce was very respectful of her parents she also felt that they were somewhat old fashioned, especially when it came to walking out with a young, or in this case, not so young, man. The alternative was for her to visit Fred, chaperoned by his mother, after much discussion this had been agreed but the best laid plans as they say, actually, it was best laid schemes according to Burns, thought Fred, but either way their plans/schemes were scuppered, although no-one was really to blame. Even so, Fred definitely got the impression that if any blame were to be apportioned it lay squarely at his door, which made him a trifle aggrieved. He had desperately wanted Joyce to visit and was as disappointed as she was, but she didn't seem to understand which had uncharacteristically annoyed him. It seemed a long time ago when he had teased her after she had written to him about the book she had been reading. As it happened Fred had also read *Gone with the Wind*, his mother had read it, and he had picked it up out of curiosity one lazy Sunday afternoon, he had thought it quite good and had surprised Joyce by quoting from it the line "You should be kissed, and often, by someone who knows what he's doing". Joyce feigned mock horror but he knew she was secretly delighted. It was when he recalled moments like that that he remembered how sweet she was, but the distance between them, both in miles and age seemed to be beginning to be taking its toll.

He knew Joyce was disappointed with him, he really hadn't given enough thought as to how they would conduct this long distance relationship, it seems a bit ridiculous to call it a romance these days! And to top it all, he had bumped into Irene the previous evening when he was out for a quick pint with Eddy and a couple of his other friends, Irene had been out walking with a girlfriend and their paths had crossed as they were on their way to the City Arms in Earlsdon. Irene had looked very fetching and very pretty in her bright summer frock, and had been delighted to see him, that was the great thing about Irene, what you saw was what you got, no side to Irene thought Fred. They had exchanged pleasantries and asked all the usual questions, how are you, your mother, yourself, your parents, your sister, your job etc! It had been lovely to catch up and as Irene and Jane went on their way, Fred remembered how easy and uncomplicated she was. It was with a somewhat heavy heart that he continued on to the pub, needless to say, he drank rather more than he usually did that evening, which no doubt had contributed to his bad mood the following morning. But as Fred was about to discover, a mild hangover was the least of his problems.

He worked steadily through the morning, although in all honesty, his mind wasn't on the job. To be fair, the mood in the office was a little subdued, a couple of the juniors had already left to join the army in anticipation of war being declared and Fred was feeling that he really must make a decision soon. His mother, of course wanted him to wait, but then she also wanted a miracle. He sighed heavily and decided to concentrate on his work, and was rather surprised to see it was almost 2pm by the time he looked up at the clock on the far wall. Fred knew his mother had packed him some lunch so he rummaged in his satchel to see what she had prepared for him, Cheese and pickle! normally this would have been perfectly adequate but today Fred fancied something a little more exciting, he would finish up and take a walk across Broadgate to the little sandwich shop come cafe were they usually had a fine selection of fillings and very tasty homemade soups. it was 2.30 by the time he had shrugged his coat on, and he was just about to step out of the office door when there was a massive explosion and then, just for a second, the world went very quiet.

Letter Thirteen

68 St Andrews Rd
Cheltenham

Sunday

Dearest Fred

You can't guess how pleased I was to speak to you this evening. This morning I spent ages trying to get through but found it was impossible – I felt pretty miserable about it – I don't know why. I'm so pleased you can come down dear – I'm afraid it's not much of a holiday for you, also I didn't give you much chance to refuse to come did I ? You do understand though don't you?

If I had thought you didn't want to come I wouldn't have pressed you, but I honestly want to spend that one week with you, I feel quite excited at the mere thought of you coming.

By the way, it's 'Cheltenham Carnival' (no rude remarks please). I must admit, you will probably think it pretty tame, I know how you dislike that sort of thing, still, it will mean a little activity throughout the town. When you write I suppose you wouldn't like to send me those photos would you?

I can't tell you how relieved I was to see on Saturday that you were ok. I had nightmares etc all that night – it might so easily have been you involved in the accident. I grabbed the first newspaper I could lay hands on and read the names of the people, I was very relieved to find you were all right.

It has been simply frantic at work this week, lots of girls have been working seven until ten in the evenings overtime – not me though. You'd be surprised, everyone seemed to want it, I guess they must have been pretty hard up. Anyhow, being so busy has left one feeling pretty limp – and what with the threat of war! A girl's fiancé in the office was called up and is supposed to be going to Egypt with the territorials. A boy, friend of the family (he comes from Coventry) came to say goodbye to us as he expects to go to France at a moment's notice with the air force.

I told mother you would be coming, she seemed quite pleased and told me there was no need to look so thrilled at the prospect of seeing you. She seems to like teasing me also – I hope I didn't interrupt this evening, if so, please apologise to Maurice for me – I won't apologise to you cos I don't think it would do you any harm! I hope you enjoy your holiday this week, endeavour to behave yourself wont you? Do you know, I haven't seen you for simply ages – I've almost forgotten what you look like , only I couldn't very well forget such a person, once having seen you.

It's getting on for time that I retired – I seem to have told you everything necessary over the phone. Except perhaps, that I'm looking forward to seeing you dear – every week that goes by I wonder if you are still as fond of me, whether you are fed up with me or not, cos you know not seeing you I don't have much hold over you, or perhaps influence would be a better word. Still I hope you won't change dear - I mustn't get morbid, must I?

Must close now.

Your own

Joyce

P.S.

I strongly disapprove of weird writing paper but had run out of other. Goodnight dear.

Fred read Joyce's letter through and then read it again, he was still in shock from the awful events of the 25th and couldn't believe how close he had been to serious injury or worst still, death. Joyce had called it an accident, but it transpired that it had been far from that. When Fred had emerged from his office and heard, and indeed, felt the explosion, he was completely bewildered as to what had happened, then people started running, some towards the source of the maelstrom, but many more away, there was a lot of confusion and people screaming, some in fear and some in pain, terrible pain.

Fred's first thought was that it had been a gas explosion, but it wasn't any accident. It transpired that the IRA had left a pushbike outside Astley's shop, parked innocently on the kerb it contained a bomb of just over 5lbs, left in the handlebar basket attached to the front of the bicycle. The carnage was dreadful, the police, who were stationed not far away were the first on the scene followed very quickly by the ambulance services. For some it was already too late, they were beyond help, five people lay dead or dying and seventy more were injured, some severely. Although Fred made a move to help if he could, he was quickly turned away by the emergency services who could see he was in no fit state to be of any use, a kindly hand directed him back to his office some of his colleagues, alerted by the explosion, took him inside, sat him down and made him drink hot sweet tea.

It was some time before the public got to know the full extent of the tragedy, it was an act of shear barbarity by the IRA. The bombing was intended 'to aid the German cause' to show a public display of strength to Germany. The irony was, it transpired, that the bomb was never supposed to be left in such a public place, it should have been left outside the police station but the IRA member who was in charge of placing the bicycle kept getting the wheels trapped in the tram lines and not onc hundred per cent sure when it would explode had panicked and left it parked on the pavement in the crowded Broadgate shopping centre.

The stories that emerged over the next few days were heartbreaking. A young woman, Elsie Ansell, just twenty-one, was caught in the centre of the blast and could only be identified by her engagement ring. A fifteen year old curly haired lad with glasses, John Arnot, full of life, who worked at W.H.Smith's died at the scene and a young trainee manager, Rex Gentle, from the same store, who happened to lodge with the youngsters family, died later from his injuries.

Gwilym Rowlands, a road sweeper, his poor wife Mary, had the grim task of identifying his body. James Clay was the oldest to die, at eighty-two, he had been having lunch with his friend in the cafe that Fred had been intending to visit, it was a regular lunchtime get-together but on this occasion James had left the cafe early because he hadn't felt well. It was the first time in six years that James and his friend had not left together.

Muriel Timms was just fourteen when her world changed forever, she was considered one of the lucky ones,she was badly injured, but survived, although she would never walk again without a limp, and the experience unsurprisingly, cast a dark shadow over the rest her life.

There were many more casualties and many stories of heroism. The emergency services worked tirelessly throughout the afternoon. Many people were in shock and just needed a gentle touch and a kind voice, but for many more life would never be the same again.

And then, as if this wasn't atrocity enough, within days it would be announced, the news that everyone had been dreading. Chamberlin had sent Hitler an ultimatum – withdraw troops from Poland or it would mean war. Germany refused and on the 3rd September Britain and France faced the inevitable and declared war on Germany.

Letter Fourteen

To say that Fred was surprised when he'd opened Joyce's latest letter
was a massive understatement. He had expected words of comfort
after what had happened earlier in the week. He had known how
worried she had been when news of the 'incident' broke, although at
the time she had thought it to be an awful accident. It was only when
the facts started to filter through that folks had realised what a terrible
tragedy had occurred. They had spoken at length on the phone and it
was clear that Joyce had been frantic with worry. Fred had felt quite
overwhelmed by her concerns and declarations of love, in many ways
it had been just what he had needed, balm for his bruised soul. He
wished desperately that he could hold her close and tell her everything
was going to be all right now, but of course, it wasn't all right, and
wasn't going to be for a long time.

In the aftermath of the tragedy Fred has declared his intention to visit Joyce regardless of any obstacles or objections, but given the fact that he was considered lucky to be alive, all disapprovals had been brushed aside. Joyce's parents had agreed for Fred to visit, they had told Joyce she must think with her head and not her heart, but as she had so succinctly put it, the head doesn't decide who the heart loves. Although he would stay in a local guest house he would be able to spend most of the time with Joyce and more importantly, her family. Evidently Joyce had been so upset at the thought of losing him that her mother and father had both put aside their worries and agreed that it was time to get to know him better.

Nevertheless, he had felt a trifle put out by her latest missive and hoped that there was nothing to worry about. He would just have to wait until Sunday.

Actually, Fred felt that he had quite a lot to think about without fretting about Joyce. The bombing in the city centre had made a lot of people realise war was inevitable and many of his friends and acquaintances were preparing to leave for training camps, both at home and abroad. Fred was definitely going to apply to join the navy, his mother was upset of course, but even she understood, no able bodied young man could seriously think of staying at home when their country needed them. The explosion had served to fuel the enthusiasm of the young and old alike and each felt it was their duty to fight for King and country more strongly than ever. A great many of the younger generation believed it would all be over by Christmas and they would march home, triumphant and bask in the glory with their tales of derring-do.

Fred also had his future with Joyce on his mind. Being so close to the dead and dying had given him pause, he wondered whether he should make the relationship more formal before he had to leave, or even, God forbid, should he walk away and let Joyce get on with her life without the worry of not knowing if he would ever come back. He knew exactly what Joyce would say, she would have no doubts at all, she would marry him and be dammed. Fred felt the same way a lot of the time but was it practical and would her parents allow it, after all Joyce would need their permission to marry as she was still considered underage. Fred actually had a chuckle to himself at the thought of Joyce's parents trying to stop her, he could well imagine the foot stamping and tearful protestations, she was quite a force when cornered.

He decided to have a talk with his mother about it, he had always valued her opinion, and considered her to be a wise and reasonable counsel so they sat down and had a long chat about the situation that evening. His mother's advice was of course very pragmatic, she listened to her son quietly, and whether she agreed with everything he said or not, she realised that decisions had to be made. They agreed between them that, as Fred was due to visit Joyce and her parents in a few days, then that would be the time to decide about any future plans. After all, Fred had not even asked Joyce if she would like to get married, or indeed engaged at such an uncertain time, and although Fred felt certain that she would, his mother said that they should at least discuss everything before making any firm plans. Also, of course, Fred needed to speak to Joyce's mother and father as she wasn't yet twenty-one, that was a conversation that Fred was not looking forward to. Although, on the surface, Fred's mother was not against Fred proposing she would very much have preferred them simply to get engaged, or have an understanding, if you will, rather than rush into marriage. In reality they still hadn't known each other that long and it was a big decision for anyone to make, war or no war. Fred was quite surprised when they had talked, the possibility of calling off the relationship had not been mentioned. He himself had not brought it up, even though he considered it one of the possibilities, and his mother had not suggested it either, perhaps thinking that if she did it would only push Fred closer into making a commitment. But Fred had thought about it. Was it really fair to ask Joyce to devote herself to him at this time, and whilst it would be lovely to know that he had someone waiting at home for him while he was away fighting, it really wasn't an ideal situation for anybody. Fred decided that his mother was right as always, he would speak to Joyce about their future and try and gauge exactly how she felt about it, and then, together, they would speak to her parents and see how they reacted. Fred had a feeling that it would not go down well, he hadn't been in Joyce's father's company much, but enough to know that he was very protective of his eldest daughter and he'd better be prepared for fireworks. Of course, thought Fred, it might be irrelevant anyway, Joyce might turn him down, with war imminent even she might feel it was not the time for romance, then again, he doubted it.

Letter Fifteen

4th September 1939

My Dear Fred

Thank you for your letter. I didn't receive it until tea time yesterday and then I had to fetch it from the sorting office. I worried and worried all Saturday morning and at 4pm in the afternoon I went into the sorting office, grabbed one of the fellows I know and asked him about it. He said the Birmingham area post had just arrived – I waited till it was sorted and received your letter. I realised you wouldn't come – I'd tried not to feel disappointed but I'm afraid I didn't succeed very well. Although now war has been declared I realise that it's best you didn't as your right place is with your people. Although of course I wish you were here. It's hateful, the place swarms with soldiers, and what with news bulletins and aeroplanes, I realise it's no good feeling frightened. The only thing is to hope it will soon be over, it seems such utter waste of life to throw it away on senseless wars. I realise this one was inevitable but that doesn't remove the realities of war does it? I thank God my father is too old to go – you're the only person I have to worry about, but I forgot you told me not to do that, didn't you – it's probably the fact that you are so far away, anything might happen to you and I shouldn't know. You might have to go and fight at a moment's notice you couldn't even say goodbye to me – it's hopeless isn't it?

I do wish dear you could come and see me soon if only for a day. Of course this probably isn't possible but if it is I do wish you would – I can't understand why this war couldn't have waited a week or two – that's being childish isn't it? It's no good me being childish now – women are more useful in emergencies.

Will you have to go back to work next week – I've still got my leave – though I guess it's not going to be a lot of use now.

We've been having hundreds of evacuation children here, we are going to have 3,500 altogether. We ourselves are meant to have soldiers if anyone, but we have sufficient family luckily. Mother was quite willing to have anyone's children whom she knew. She also wondered about you, whether your people would want to move to a safer place?

I don't know when you'll get this letter perhaps one from you will cross with it – but I felt I had to write to you. It's rotten luck isn't it but I guess it affects most people the same don't you? It seems impossible that we are at work doesn't it. When I think about it and realise what it means I feel terrified. I feel like I should like you to take me in your arms and tell me it's going to be all right. I meant to write you a cheerful letter but I'm afraid I haven't been very successful. Last night we had a terrific thunderstorm to add to the tense atmosphere and I lay in bed and thought it wouldn't be half so bad if you were with me – the solution to my problem would be (not to fall in love with someone so far away) – it's a bit late now to rectify it.

Fred dear, I did want to see that new sports jacket of yours – maybe you'll wear it next time I see you (I had a new frock in honour of your coming – just think what you have missed).

I must go now dear please write to me soon as I shall be waiting to hear from you. Try and get down to see me if you can won't you dear? Cos Joyce gets very lonely with no one to kiss her goodnight.

Really must close

Your very own

Joyce

It was a sad letter thought Fred, but he hadn't been surprised by that. Joyce had been bitterly disappointed that the planned break together had been cancelled but at least she had understood why. It was an incredibly difficult time. War had been declared, and whilst many folk were being rather stoical, a good few others wondered if they would see many more summers. Although the youth of the country felt optimistic, believing as had been said many times, it would all be over by Christmas, the older generation knew it could be a long and bloody battle.

Fred had decided that he needed to visit Joyce as soon as possible, he desperately needed to see her and if he didn't go soon he might miss his chance altogether. He was determined to try for the navy, but if that wasn't possible then he would join the army along with many of his friends. He had asked for a few days off but as he'd just had his annual leave he was told it wasn't possible so they would just have to make do with a couple of days over the weekend. He knew that Joyce would be delighted, even just to see him for a few hours, he felt, despite the war, that they were on the verge of something wonderful. It was now clear to him that Joyce loved him unconditionally and he was taken a little by surprise to realise that he felt the same way.

Fred had told his mother that he intended to propose to Joyce when he next saw her and his mother had, much as Fred had expected, expressed a little concern. After all, she had not even met her intended daughter in law, but these were strange times and she conceded that she would have to trust her son's judgment. Fred had gone down to the coach station and had managed to book himself on a coach for the following Saturday, he would only be able to stay one night but that had to be better than nothing. Joyce had burst into tears when they had spoken on the phone and he had told her his news, she was absolutely thrilled and told him she couldn't wait to see him and touch him. He would be able to see her in her new dress after all, and he would wear his new sports jacket wouldn't he? They would make a frightfully attractive couple and would turn heads wherever they went, at least that's what Joyce thought. Fred was immensely cheered by the conversation and found himself smiling broadly as he hung up the phone. She really was a complete delight.

The rest of the week passed by in a blur, the city was very busy, there was, unsurprisingly, a sense of emergency in the air. Families gathered together and friends huddled in groups, all the talk was of Hitler and war and what the future might hold. It was a miserable feeling, but at the same time there was a sense of excitement, as if something extraordinary was about to happen and Fred felt quite lightheaded as he boarded his bus early on the Saturday morning, amidst all of the fear and confusion, a feeling of hope prevailed.

Letter Sixteen

68 St Andrews Rd
Cheltenham

Monday

Dearest Fred

Thanks so much for your letter dear I received it this morning – not bad considering the war and Coventry's postal services? I'm sorry to hear you were so tired on Sunday, perhaps it was the result of being 'dragged about so much down here' do you think so? I thought of you going back to the daily grind this morning I guess it came rather hard.

I suggested that I should have my leave in a few weeks time to my supervisor – actually it was an unfortunate time to choose as she had been weeping all the morning over a quarrel she had had with one of the monitors. Why our exchanges can't leave each other alone and live in peace amazes me. With reference to the leave she said "it was hard to say in these difficult times" I'm going to put it in a paper which will be dealt with by the P.M. This should simplify matters. I can't think that forthcoming events will make such an enormous change now that we are actually at war. I shall have to explain to Miss Cartwright that it is no good her offering me leave at one or two days notice. What the above woman really needs is a husband who would defiantly ill-treat her and boss her around. She's cut out for such an environment, but as a supervisor she's hopeless.

What about the books you were going to send me to improve my intellectual knowledge. I thought your friend Bill sounded very nice. You know Fred, I don't think your friends would approve of me at all. I think they'd consider me rather school-

girlish. I should hate that to happen. I'm not half nice enough for you in lots of ways – you realise that don't you?

We all decided that we missed you when you left. Mother sends her love – I guess she is fonder of you than you think – I am rather sure she is after a conversation she had with me yesterday. I think the idea of a walk with you once a week would be wonderful – still, it's not the people who are content with a little who always get what they deserve.

I haven't been carrying my gas-mask about with me and we haven't had any air-raids yet, plenty of time though for things like that. You might remember me to Bob and tell him I think it's rotten luck about his girlfriend in Leamington. He's rather unfortunate isn't he? Still as you say 10 miles is not 55. I do hope dear I'll be able to come to Coventry for those few days somehow I've got a feeling inside me I'll come. I've no doubt that I'll be frightfully nervous but as it's time I got over such foolishness that won't do me any harm. I do hope you will get this tomorrow as I know you'll expect it. I shan't get a chance to ring up until next Sunday, at least it's not probable but don't be surprised if I do – after all the unexpected normally happens.

Must close now.

All my love.

Your

Joyce

It had been a strange couple of days Fred had thought as he dressed for work on Monday morning. His mother had been waiting up for him when he finally got home on Sunday. It was quite late and he was very tired but nevertheless they had sat and had tea and toast and chewed over the events of the last forty eight hours. As determined as Fred had been to propose to Joyce, it somehow never quite happened, the afternoon and evening had passed in a blur, Joyce was so pleased to see him, she barely gave him chance to speak. Also, he had wanted to talk to Joyce's father first and he had proved to be particularly elusive. Fred wasn't sure if this was by accident or design, but it was almost impossible to speak to him alone. The odd times when they were together it had been impossible to engage him in conversation and in any case Fred was not confident of a positive outcome. He definitely had the impression that Mr Wright wasn't altogether convinced that this rather earnest young man was the best thing for his obviously love-struck young daughter. Fred could completely understand and would no doubt had felt the same had he been in his position. Times were hard enough as it was without thinking of marriage and the obvious problem that it would bring with it. The result was that Fred did not discuss the possibility with Mr Wright or Joyce. Knowing how headstrong she could be, it would be better, he decided, to leave all talk of the future until another time.

Joyce had dragged him all over the town and then there had been a family meal, which, to say the least, Fred had found rather uncomfortable. He seemed to get on well with Joyce's mother and younger sister but her father was quite a cold fish.

The one good thing to come out of the visit is that Joyce's parents had agreed that she could travel to Coventry for a few days and stay with Fred and his mother, with the proviso that Fred's mother would contact them personally to confirm her approval. Joyce had started to make her plans immediately and if Fred was honest with himself he felt slightly overwhelmed by it all. A part of him had been relieved, in many respects, that he had not actually got around to asking for Joyce's hand. When he had discussed it with his mother she had been quite pleased, there would be plenty of time for all that she said, if it's meant to be it's meant to be. Fred had the feeling that she had given a huge sigh of relief when she finally climbed the stairs for bed.

Joyce had said in her last letter that she was hoping to get the train into Leamington Spa, and Bob had stepped up to offer his services and pick her up from the station. He was a good egg Bob. It all hinged on Joyce's supervisor really, whom Joyce had been, uncharacteristically, rather mean about. Even so, knowing Joyce as he did, he was quite sure that she would move heaven and earth to get to see him.

Fred had been making plans of his own as it happened, he had finally decided that he was definitely going to apply to join the Navy. It was a big decision and his mother was unhappy with his choice and couldn't understand his hurry. He would be called soon enough she said, could he not just wait and see what happens. But Fred was determined, most of his friends were already thinking about what they wanted to do, some had already signed up, Fred wanted to be patriotic and felt that he must show his support for his King and country. He would mention it in his next letter to Joyce as it was important to let her know his plans as well. He hoped she would be pragmatic about it and be more understanding than his mother.

It was with a weary heart that Fred sat down to breakfast that morning, things had not gone quite as expected on his trip to Cheltenham. It was not that he had been disappointed, and although it had been lovely to see Joyce and he had got to spend some time with the family, something felt out of place. He was probably just tired he thought. It felt a very tiring time. He had hoped that things would seem clearer after a good night's sleep, but if anything, it had merely served to have muddied the waters.

Letter Seventeen

68 St Andrews Rd
Cheltenham

Thursday

Dearest Fred

*Thanks for your letter, I didn't receive it until tea time today.
Dearest do you realise I can have my leave (also a half day on
Saturday) on the week commencing 25th Sept: that is a week
on Saturday – will it be O.K. for me to come – I guess the railway
still runs. I shall endeavour to come on Saturday cos you won't
have to work on Sunday will you? Also you could probably meet
me – logic isn't it? Actually mother is now being awkward, she
says I can't come unless your mother definitely invites me
(meaning a written invitation I presume). Really mothers can
be trying can't they? Anyhow I'll talk to you about it on Sunday.
Honestly Fred it seems things are always going to be against
us. If I wasn't so keen on you and about coming to see you I
guess I should just quit trying to come to Coventry. Still I must
keep my chin up and if it's ok your end I see no reason why I
shouldn't come. I think I've explained it all quite clearly. I'll try
and ring up 11.50 am – if I find this is unsuitable I'll find some
way of letting you know, O.K.? It seems such ages since you
were here dear. The town is simply overrun with soldiers – I'm
sorry to hear your mother is taking such an unsympathetic view
about you joining the navy – personally I should hate you to
join anything and have to go away but I realise it's better to
know about these things than to live with the uncertainty of
the knowledge that any moment one may be called upon to go.*

*I feel sorry for your mother she must love you very much. Still
much as I love you I wouldn't really wish you to stay in safety
when it was your duty to do otherwise. In this respect wars hit
women more than men. Still I'm being morbid now – and I ought*

to cheer you up. It's nice to think I'll be seeing you soon isn't it dear? I can't write much more as it's nearly bedtime. I'm getting quite thrilled at the prospect of visiting Coventry. Hoping to hear you on Sunday at 11.50.

You know you have all my love don't you?

Your own

Joyce

(It's nice to be someone's (own) isn't it?)

So, it was more or less settled, thought Fred as he read Joyce's latest missive. She was determined to visit Coventry when she was on leave. It was arranged that she would travel by train to Leamington Spa and Bob would pick him up and take him to meet her. Fred was a little surprised that her parents had agreed to the visit, although his mother still needed to write and confirm that she was also happy to have Joyce to stay. It would be nice to have her stay for a week, Fred reflected, although he did wonder how he would be able to keep her entertained. He would have to think of places they could go sightseeing together. His mother was also looking forward to the visit as she was eager to meet the young lady who had apparently stolen her boy's heart. It had to be said though, that she had felt recently that Fred was not quite as committed as he had been. She knew her son well and had begun to feel a little shadow of doubt creeping in when he had talked about her.

When Fred had returned from his trip to Cheltenham previously she had waited for him to announce that they were engaged, but no announcement was forthcoming and whilst she was curious but didn't pry, she felt that Fred had seemed to be somewhat withdrawn over the following week and she that there was definitely something amiss. But, to be fair, it was a difficult time all round. Damn bloody war!

Fred's mother decided to sit down and write to Joyce's mother later that evening, just a few lines to let her know that she would be delighted to welcome Joyce into her home and looked forward to finally meeting her. She must get the box room ready and air the bedding, she would buy some flowers to make the room look a little prettier, it would be nice to have a young lady to stay, they could have some lovely walks together and possibly an afternoon tea in one of the parks, of course, it would all depend on the weather but at the moment it was looking quite promising.

When Fred came in from work later, they had a chat about what they might be able to plan for the visit. The New Hippodrome theatre had been completed in 1937, and it was an impressive sight. It was the third Hippodrome to be opened in Coventry, it had opened it's doors on Monday the 1st of November 1937 with Harry Roy and his Band and, amongst several other acts, the twelve New Hippodrome Lovelies presented by Max Rivers. It was built on a grand scale and a was much more spacious and luxurious theatre than the previous one, the folk of Coventry were extremely proud of it. Fred's mother told him to pop out and get a late edition of the *Midland Daily Telegraph* and have a look at the shows planned for the next few weeks, a trip to the theatre was definitely on the cards. In fact, she thought, even if Joyce didn't want to go, she might just treat herself.

By the time they had finished supper they had quite an itinerary planned and Fred seemed a lot more cheerful. He helped his mother with the dishes and then said he was going to change and meet up with Bob and Tom for a couple of pints at Ma Cooper's. His mother would sit and write her letter she said. She told Fred to give her best to the boys and settled down with her writing paper and the radio.

Letter Eighteen

68 St Andrews Rd
Cheltenham

Dearest Fred

Thanks for your letter dear I received it this morning. After a great deal of bother I think I've managed to get off duty at 1pm on Saturday. There is sure to be a train sometime after that on Saturday isn't there? So all being well I'll arrive on Saturday evening, at least we'll hope so – I won't be able to let you know definitely until Thursday or Friday – but I'll either phone you or send a telegram. I went to tea with Rachel yesterday and we went (like two good girls) to chapel. You know there's a bit of good to be got out of a religious service especially at a time like this.

I've been fetching apples for mother most of the evening. Also having a frock fitted – its skin tight, I trust you'll approve. By the way I was told by an old friend of mother's that she hardly recognised me I was so grown up – and also so lady-like! I thought you'd be pleased to know – it must be your good influence on me. Actually I don't feel at all lady-like or grown up – sometimes I feel just – well, exactly the same as I did when I left school. Of course I'm a lot different really.

It's awfully good of Bob to offer his services I should very much like to see him again. I will do as you say and book thro' to Leamington Spa and you will meet me there ok? Do you think you will recognise me after all this time – I suppose you still want me to come and visit you?

You know Fred you write very business-like letters

(Tues) Just this moment I received a letter from your mother – Will post a reply with this. She must be very sweet cos it's a

sweet letter. By the way it's morning now and I'm due at work very soon so must go – will communicate with you again very soon.

Must close now

All my love

Your own

Joyce

P.S.

If it gets much colder I shall have to bring my winter woolies with me shan't I?

Fred was feeling a little more positive as he read Joyce's latest correspondence, he was looking forward to the visit now after having some doubts as to whether it was a good idea. It had all seemed so simple when they were in Skegness, but now it seemed so much more complicated. He knew that his mother was very curious about his recent visit to Cheltenham, he also felt that he wasn't yet ready to discuss it. In fact he was starting to feel quite overwhelmed by it all, partly because of Joyce's growing dependence on him and partly because of the war. His mother was being very patient and was plainly trying to smooth the way by planning all sorts of outings and treats for himself and Joyce when finally she arrived. Bob had been good enough to offer his services regarding picking Joyce up from the station in Leamington Spa, in fact he was looking forward to a jaunt out in his little Austin ten, people didn't tend to go far from home these days so it would be an adventure if nothing else. They were going to set off early and have a walk round the town first, maybe stop and have a jar or two at a local hostelry. He had heard that the Talbot was a pleasant watering hole.

The week, in fact, passed by in a blur. They had picked Joyce up from the station and driven straight to Fred's house so that his mother could make her acquaintance. Fred was, to his surprise, a little nervous about the meeting but Joyce had looked delightful in a rather grown up suit that made her look surprisingly mature. She wore her blonde hair up and a little make-up to bring out the colour of her eyes. Fred felt quite proud to escort her up to the front door where his mother was waiting patiently. They hit it off straightaway. Joyce was charming and appreciative, thanking his mother in advance for a lovely stay, and his mother took an immediate liking to Joyce who was so excited to finally be in Coventry, it was infectious.

They had a lovely week, visiting local places of interest and even managing the long walk to Kenilworth to see the castle, they both had blisters after that.

Joyce and his mother also had an afternoon out together, though what they discussed was never mentioned to Fred, which was absolutely fine by him. Fred had to admit that they did have a wonderful time, it was always the same when they were actually together, it was the distance between them that caused him to doubt his feelings, but now was not the time for folk to be uprooting themselves. Fred was also very aware that Joyce's parents would, quite rightly, he felt, thoroughly disapprove of any serious commitment in the present climate, although he had the distinct impression that his mother would be exactly the opposite and thoroughly approve.

The week's visit accumulated with a trip to the New Coventry Hippodrome Theatre where they went to see the Variety Show. Joyce was very impressed with the theatre itself, it was really quite opulent and grand. Joyce said she felt like a princess as they wandered trough the lobby on their way to the seats. It was a fantastic show, lots of music and comedy with a cast that included Rawicz and Landauer, Douglas Byng and Oliver Wakefield among others. They had had an ice cream each in the interval and laughed when Fred dropped some down his shirt front. Joyce made a great fuss of wiping it off and scolding him for his clumsiness. Just like an old married couple, thought Fred.

Joyce had written to her mother as soon as they had got home from the theatre, even though she was due to go home herself the following day, she had wanted to tell her all about the evening whilst it was still fresh she said. Their last evening together was rather sad, they had both got used to being together, especially as Fred's mother was more understanding than Joyce's parents and allowed them to have a little more privacy than they were afforded in Cheltenham. Fred was definitely feeling that there was a future for them after all, if it wasn't for the dammed war he might have proposed right there and then, but caution prevented him from losing complete control of his emotions.

Bob was to pick them up at 9am on the Saturday morning and take them both over to Leamington Spa so Joyce could catch her train. Tommy had decided to join the party and go along for the ride, a decision he would come to regret. It was a rather bittersweet parting for them both, with each of them promising to write soon, and Joyce imploring Fred to try and visit as soon as possible. Fred was more than happy to comply and promised to make arrangement that very day. He waved Joyce off until they could no longer see each other and then returned to Bob and Tommy who had kept a discreet distance whilst Joyce and Fred had said their goodbyes. Good chaps, both of them.

The trip back to Coventry was a little over ten miles, they were about half way when the accident happened.

Letter Nineteen

68 St Andrews Rd
Cheltenham

Monday

Dearest Fred

I can't tell you how sorry I am about the accident – I'm very thankful that <u>you</u> are not hurt – of course I'm glad the others of your party were not hurt. Perhaps you would convey my regrets to Bob cos I feel that it was indirectly my fault. I do hope it will all go off ok, don't let it worry you will you dear? It seems unfortunate after such a marvellous week doesn't it? Still, I wouldn't have missed last week for anything. I'm going to write a short note to your mother. You know I wrote to my mother on Friday she received the letter this morning. Pretty good isn't it? It seems so funny not to have you around – I had just got used to having you constantly about. Having you advising me and telling me what to do etc. I appreciate it now I no longer have it! I've no doubt you'll be glad to have a week's decent sleep.

It's rotten having to work after a week's holiday I'd grown accustomed to being a lady leading a lazy life of ease (tea in bed etc) I miss that too. Still I guess you're not in the mood for reading letters after a knock up like that. Dearest I really can't tell you how sorry I am – must close now, try and drop me a line soon won't you dear.

All my love

Your own

Joyce

83

It had all been rather stupid thought Fred, why on earth Bob had let Tommy take the wheel he would never comprehend. Tommy hadn't passed his driving test so was sadly lacking a full licence and although he had been learning to drive he was not used to a busy main road like the Kenilworth Road. They had motored quite happily through Kenilworth and were just coasting down Crackley Hill when, completely unexpectedly a muntjac suddenly shot across the road from the bushes on the right hand side. A more experienced driver would have had trouble avoiding it, let alone poor old Tommy who panicked and swerved straight into the undergrowth. Fortunately for the startled occupants of the car it was quite a soft landing, they somehow managed to avoid any of the many trees along the edge and settled with a thud into a massive blackberry bush. Not so fortunately, it seemed that a police car had been following closely behind and had witnessed the whole thing first hand. This, of course, would not normally have been a problem, it was quite obvious that it was a genuine accident which couldn't have been avoided. Only problem was Tommy had no L plates on the car and, to add salt to the wound, foolishly they had stopped off at the Talbot Inn for a quick pint or two before setting off home to Coventry. As shaken and bruised and relieved as they were that there was no real damage done, they all knew, that right now that was the least of their troubles.

The police pulled in behind them and got out to check if everyone was alright, they were very solicitous at first and very concerned that everyone was unharmed more than anything else. After checking on the occupants and establishing there was no serious injuries they asked Tommy to try and reverse the car back onto the road if possible which is when he started to panic, he had so much trouble trying to find reverse gear that the older of the two policemen, assuming he was in shock, decided to do it for him. It must have been during the crossover as Tommy stepped out of the car and the policeman went to slide behind the wheel that he caught the faint whiff of Fullers best on Tommy's breath. That's when they asked for his driving licence. Poor old Bob, trapped in the passenger seat due to an oversized bush making it impossible for him to open the door, put his head in his hands and groaned. Now they were for it.

The two officers were actually quite good about the whole thing, and possibly a little amused. Tommy was to report to Coventry police station the following Monday, and it was suggested that Bob joined him as it was his car. Fred, sitting in the back with a bloody nose due to hitting the back of Bob's head on impact was of course completely innocent even though it had been his idea to go for a drink in the first place. They managed to get the car back onto the road without too much fuss and allowed Bob, who thankfully, and rather unusually, had only indulged in a lemonade, to take the wheel so they could get back to town, the car was slightly battered down the left hand side and more so at the front which had taken the full force but still roadworthy. It was a very sheepish threesome that made their way home that afternoon.

When they finally limped into Earlsdon all three of them were feeling a bit bruised and battered and a little sorry for themselves. Not particularly wishing to face his mother straightaway, knowing full well that she would have more than a few words to say on the subject, especially the fact that they had stopped off for a drink, Fred suggested that they popped to Ma Cooper's for a beer, purely medicinal of course, for the shock! Unfortunately Fred's mother was already at the door. She took in the state of the car and the forlorn faces of the occupants and nodded. With pursed lips she ushered all three of them into the kitchen were she started to make hot sweet tea. Whilst she busied herself with the crockery she also told Fred and his friends what they already knew. How could they have been so silly! Fancy letting Tommy drive! They could all have been killed! Wasn't it time that they all grew up! Didn't they realise there was a war on? Fred and his friends sat quietly, suitable chastened, unable to argue. Then she turned with a softer smile, and said thank goodness they were all right and to drink their tea while its was hot. Fred sipped from the scalding cup and smiled quietly to himself, of course she was absolutely right, but war or no war, and accidents aside, he couldn't help but remember the glorious week he had just spent with his girl.

Letter Twenty

68 St Andrews Rd
Cheltenham

Friday

Dear Fred

Thanks for your letter, I received it yesterday – I'm relieved to hear you're all so far ok. I gathered from your writing that you were pretty shook up by it. What you really wanted was someone to make a fuss of you, a good idea don't you think? I'm sorry you had an accident cos it meant you hadn't time to miss me. I wanted you to miss me and think it was different – the added excitement wouldn't leave you time for that would it? Still I missed you – I feel as though I had been back in Cheltenham for weeks – everything is so ordinary. So the same, no excitement or thrill attached to life at all. This I suppose is the expected reaction to an enjoyable holiday. You know I like having a male around to escort me about – especially when it's you. It's been frightfully dark in the black-out round here – the best thing to do is to stay indoors in the evenings. I admit it's not very interesting.

I'm sorry about your mother dear – you know you do talk to her rather on the (rough guy) side dear. Still I admit it must be trying, But then as you would say all women are obstinate. I don't wholly agree with you, men are just as obstinate but they've got no-one to tell them so. Still I'll tell you so someday – if you need it – of course.

I still think you're frightfully businesslike on the phone at your office. Having spoken to you I get the impression that you don't care a hang for me and that I'm rather a nuisance. I then wonder why I care for you when you appear so uninterested. Of course this is my imagination which at times is pretty vivid. I can often imagine awful things happening when there is no need. I must get out of this 'habit'. I try and realise that you have to be like that at work but it doesn't make me feel any different. Still your letter reassures me, it's so much like you and I can remember such a lot of things about you. Every time I see you I have a few more things to associate with you.

If I write to you like this I shall start to get morbid which I mustn't do – I must remember I have to cheer you up. Do you realise Fred dear you haven't teased me just lately – perhaps you don't love me anymore? I think you'd better tell me again. By the way dear I don't suppose you'll get this epistle until Monday, so I shall probably have spoken to you on Sunday at 3pm. Mother sends you her love – I can't see that you need any more love – I should have thought mine was sufficient – still maybe it wouldn't do you any harm. You like a lot of fuss don't you darling?

I must go now and face the black-out alone down to the General – I can't say I like trotting about in the deep darkness nevertheless for you I would brave even that (a noble speech isn't it ?)

Goodnight dear

All my love

Joyce

Fred had indeed spoken to Joyce on the Sunday before her letter arrived, it had been a rather stilted conversation. He had to admit, if only to himself, that he may had exaggerated the severity of the 'accident' that they had had on the way back from the station when he told Joyce about it. He didn't really know why and regretted it now, but she had gone on a bit about her visit and how wonderful it had been and how much she loved being with him that he had tried to change the direction of the conversation, and found himself embellishing somewhat. It was true that Fred had had a perfectly lovely time as well, but had to admit to himself that he was almost relieved when it was time for Joyce to return to Cheltenham. He did wonder if it was because he felt that he was being forced to make a decision that he was no longer sure was the right one for him. Joyce had obviously picked up on this. When all said and done she was a very perceptive young lady. He had felt bad after he had read her latest letter or epistle as she preferred to call them, he even went out and bought her a small gift, very inexpensive but very Joyce, and posted to her straightway.

His mother, sensing the atmosphere, was keeping her own counsel. She had had her say concerning the silly accident, poor Tommy had had his fingers well and truly rapped at the police station but luckily they were taking no further action as Tommy was due to start his training any day now. That was the other problem, thought Fred gloomily, what was he to do in the war? His mother was still unhappy about him volunteering but Fred desperately wanted to do his bit and they had had words which was very unusual and didn't sit well with either of them. Then, as always, his mind wandered back to Joyce. She was in love and had told him so on numerous occasions over the last week, and he had promised her he felt the same, but it was becoming more and more difficult for him. Whenever he was with her it was easy to believe in a happy ending, but as soon as they parted it was becoming increasingly effortless for him to be single and carefree again. Was it only a few months ago that life was so much more simple? Did he really want a lifetime with Joyce? Fred felt that if he had to question his feelings then the answer was no, but at the same time, was it simply the fear of the future, with all the horror of war and the distance between them it was neither the time or the place to be considering romance.

They had parted rather sweetly with declarations of affection and promises to meet again soon but it was getting to be almost impossible to arrange. Fred also had the feeling that, not just Joyce, but her parents also, were looking for a positive commitment from him which he was seemingly more and more reluctant to make. If he were to propose, thought Fred, then it must be because he felt it was one hundred per cent the right thing to do, and not because it was simply now expected of him.

Letter Twenty One

68 St Andrews Rd
Cheltenham

Thursday

Dearest Fred

Thanks for your letter I received it this morning. I'm glad to hear that you miss me? Just a little! I'm pretty fed up with life at the moment – there is nothing to do and no-one to do it with!

Last night I went to the flicks with Rachel Green, the film was marvellous 'Wuthering Heights' – frightfully emotional and sad. I just sat and wept, I honestly couldn't help it – it seemed to tear you inside – if you know what I mean – I must confess that I am fond of passionate dramatic tales. Maybe I'm what you would call 'kind of soft' – still if it hasn't been to Coventry (it's a fairly recent film) I strongly advise you to see it. We could then compare reactions ?

I don't seem to have heard from you for ages – our letters seem far between don't they ? I don't know how you feel, but at times I feel that for all I hear or see of you I might just as well never have met you. Of course I realise the war mucks these things up. But not being very angelic – I get frightfully impatient. I'm sorry to bother you writing stuff like this but I'm afraid I'm made a little bit that way. If I was making anything I always wanted to get it finished right away – I like things that show immediate results. Now I'm older I realise that this can't always be so. But you realise don't you that this is why I feel rather impatient sometimes.

Anyhow, my letter writing must be improving.

Haven't been able to get any nice samples of wool (those I got weren't very nice) cos I've been working late. Shall have to enclose them in my next epistle by the way, how much do you measure round the chest? I ought to know (just right for me to put my arms around).

As regards Sunday Fred dear – I'm sorry I won't be able to ring you dear – I'm working until 1.30 in the morning – and the 'male' who puts me through isn't 'on' in the afternoon. I don't particularly want to ask another person as it's apt to get rather involved if too many people get mixed up. You see my point dearest don't you? I would if I could but I can't – if anything crops up and I can I'll send you a wire – will that be ok? I shall attempt to ring you tomorrow if things aren't to busy.

Also on Sunday afternoon Rachel and I are going to help Mrs Tyler with some evacuee babies. I don't quite know how we'll get on – but I'm hoping. I thought your letter was very good. Quite an improvement on some. By the way I'm getting very attached to the china rabbit you bought me, I call it 'Charlie' – it isn't exactly like you (that would be too complimentary to the rabbit) nevertheless I'm awfully fond of it. I see it last thing at night and first thing in the morning – the next best thing to having you (first and last).

Must go to the post now, it's not such a nice letter as I'd have liked it to be – I've got a headache and want making a fuss of – unfortunately I have to make a fuss of myself – must go dearest.

All my love

Joyce

Please write soon won't you!

P.S. I forgot to mention it but I love you.

It was with a slightly heavy heart that Fred had read Joyce's latest letter, she did sound fed up bless her. He had to admit that his letters had tailed off somewhat, there always seemed something else to occupy him these days! He was, in fact, still trying to decide what to do with his life. Tommy was due to start his army training in Oswestry the following week and Fred was still dithering. His mother was saying very little but her body language spoke volumes. The full horror of war was starting to hit home. The HMS Royal Oak had been torpedoed in Scarpa Flow off the Orkneys in Scotland a few days before by a German U boat and it had sent shock waves around the country. More than eight hundred men and boys had lost their lives out of a complement of twelve hundred and people were finally realising that it wasn't a game.

Fred was still trying to work out what to do about Joyce, not so long ago he had had it all mapped out, or so he thought, but now he wasn't so sure. He knew he cared for her and really enjoyed her company when they were together but it was becoming increasingly easy to put her to one side when they were apart. She had a knack of making him feel inadequate at times and he didn't know why. Fred felt that she thought that she was far more committed to the relationship than he was, which had the ring of truth to it, but the more she pushed him on their future together the more he felt himself backing away. He was almost starting to dread the post landing on the hall floor. The idea of him having to choose wool samples so she could knit him a pullover was quite alarming and he was beginning to wish he hadn't sent her that silly china rabbit now. It was only a small thing but as usual she had blown it out of all proportion. Lord only knows when he would be able to see her again, the prospect of travelling anywhere at the moment was daunting to say the least.

Fred decided to put Joyce and her letter to one side for the time being, he was going out with his chums later and needed to get ready, so he folded up her letter and popped it in his draw with the others. They were going to Ma Cooper's for drinks and darts, primarily to give Tommy a bit of a send off before he started his training, but also, they all felt like they needed to let their hair down and just be the lads for an evening; it had been a while thought Fred.

Letter Twenty Two

68 St Andrews Rd
Cheltenham

Sunday

Dearest Fred

I really must write to you. I've no doubt you'll write to me today – at least I hope you will. It's simply poured with rain all day, have stayed in all afternoon and evening knitting and writing letters etc. We also entertained Elsie's boyfriend to tea. He's quite a sweet infant really. By the way I managed to procure some very small cuttings of wool – I went to about half a dozen shops and selected the best from amongst them. I hope you'll approve of one of them dear and let me know so that I can commence.

Haven't done anything interesting since I last wrote – oh I bought some 'superior' pyjamas but that wouldn't interest you would it?

By the way I've parted my hair in the middle – mother doesn't like it but it's a change if nothing else.

It seemed funny not ringing you up dearest. Still I guess you went out with the boys instead. Remember me to Bob and tell him I hope he's no worse for his accident. How's life going with you – I trust your people are well? Please give them my love. Dearest it seems ages since I was there with you all – I only wish I was now. I don't suppose there is any likelihood of you coming down in the near future, its pretty hopeless isn't it? How I hate the war for all this. I want to live and laugh and enjoy life and somehow it doesn't seem possible these days. I'm getting almost as pessimistic as you get morbid. I just want making a fuss of. I think I'll pop up for the evening providing you'll be very nice to me. Would you?

One of the girls at work is marrying a lifeguard in nine weeks time, there's a new regulation in the civil service – and telephonists can get married and continue working on condition that their temporary employment terminates at the end of the war. This female is going to do this and there is quite an excitement at the office. I feel quite jealous! Not really of course, but all we hear all day is "My Jamie this and my Jamie that" etc.

Mother sends her love and of course I send just a little of mine. My only regret is that I could love you a lot nicer if I had you to hand.

Still one day I will and then I'll be awful nice to you – I even offered to let mother go to church some Sunday mornings whilst I cook the dinner, it would be good practise wouldn't it?

I must close now will write again soon.

All my love

Your own

Joyce

P.S.

Don't mix two lumps of wool together cos they're from different shops.

Fred had not replied to Joyce's letter straightaway, it was a couple of days before he sat down to apply himself to the task in hand, he was sad to think that that was how he felt, that it was a task. He used to so look forward to reading and replying to her letters. Actually, it had also been the result of an enormous hangover. They had indeed 'tied one on' as the expression goes, when they had gone out a couple of nights previous. Tommy had certainly had a send off he wouldn't forget. The City Arms had been crowded and the atmosphere quite jolly as folk just wanted to let themselves go and have some fun. The friends had got caught up in the pervading mood and drank far more than they would have done normally. The evening had ended with a sing song round the old piano and they even managed an after-hours drink courtesy of the manageress because of Tommy's impending departure. Fred had very little recollection of the walk home but felt sure it had involved more than one hedge and judging by the bruise on his forehead, most definitely a lamp post!

Joyce's last letter had not filled him with much joy at all, she had mentioned that another one of her friends was getting married and she had said that she felt jealous, which Fred took, rightly or wrongly, as a bit of a dig at him. He was a bit alarmed as well about how her cooking dinner was good practise, good practise for what he wondered. Joyce was obviously feeling a bit down and the possibility of them meeting anytime soon was not on the cards. Fred sighed, and decided to try and make an effort.

He had learnt of something that he thought Joyce would find very interesting. The holiday camp in Skegness where he had been staying when they first met had been requisitioned by the Government. The rumour was that is was going to be used as a POW camp so there would actually be Germans living in his chalet, it was crazy he thought, it seemed only a short time ago that the place had been full of such fun and laughter and the world had seemed full of possibilities. It had only been five months since they had met but right now it seemed like a life time away. Fred also told Joyce about Tommy's send off and the raucous evening that they had all enjoyed. He used the inevitable results of his overindulgence as his reason for his sloppy reply to her letter and apologised for the consequences. She would like that, he thought with a wry smile. Fred also needed to make an effort with the wool samples, he really wasn't bothered one way or the other about a hand knitted pullover but if it made Joyce happy so be it, it really was quite kind of her to want to do it, although he had no idea of her expertise in that department!

He thanked her for asking after his family, such as it was, and sent his sincerest regards to her mother, father and sister Elsie, he even extended his felicitations to Elsie's boyfriend. Fred read the letter back and decided, that all things considered, he had done a reasonable job.

Fred ended the letter with much love, he still felt undecided about the future, but after all, he thought, what harm could there be in him writing to an attractive young girl when there was almost no chance of seeing her again this year. Who knows what the future would bring, he might as well just go along with it for now, there was no real harm in it after all he said to himself, but even Fred wasn't sure he believed that!

Letter Twenty Three

68 St Andrews Rd
Cheltenham

19th October 1939

Dear Fred

Thank you for your letter. How are you? It's been lovely here today. I had a half day and Rachel and I went for a walk up the common and got lots of leaves

We met thousands of soldiers, some stopped a lorry and said "Taxi miss" can't you imagine us accepting a ride in an army lorry – not us, we're far too superior. I've been going to tap dancing again, it's as a good a form of exercise as any. I look frightfully sweet in a very brief green affair. Father says I look like a baby gazelle – all legs. I'm afraid he doesn't appreciate me – I wonder if you would.

I felt quite affected when I read your letter especially your reference to Skegness – somehow it made me want to cry – I don't know why? It seems such a long time ago doesn't it?

I hate the idea of Germans in your chalet don't you? I wonder if our ghosts haunt it occasionally. How's Coventry getting on these days? Does your mother still go shopping at teatime and stay out in the black-out? Shall try and ring you up on Sunday but will drop you a line later on in the week. What do you think about the war – I'm disquieted with the whole business. We were hanging on line yesterday preliminary to air raid warnings for some time – but nothing came of it. Even an air raid warning (without the raid) would be welcome it would be exciting wouldn't it. I just feel in the mood for adventure, I'd like to do something really thrilling. I guess I shall get rid of the feeling in the night. I must go now darling and catch the post. Will write again later

All my love

Your own

Joyce

P.S.

Please write soon dearest

Your own Joyce

They had spoken on the Sunday, Fred was quite surprised by how pleased he was to hear her voice after so long. He had been seriously down in the dumps for the last week or more. His job was causing him concern, there was talk of "having to let people go" although Fred couldn't see why, the work still seemed to be there although the overtime had dried up in recent weeks. One or two of the lads had been talking about leaving the country altogether, partly to avoid receiving their call up papers and partly to make a new start away from the threat of bombs. Some would have called it cowardly though others would have thought it brave, making a whole new start on the other side of the world. He had talked to Joyce about the possibility of going to America and she was surprisingly supportive, but, of course she would be, she expected to go with him, and Fred, to his shame, hadn't disillusioned her. In fact he had told her that he loved her for the first time in ages and the conversation had got very emotional and intense. He actually felt quite guilty after they had said their goodbyes and hung up. Fred was well aware that Joyce would need her parents permission to travel to America, married or not, and he was also well aware that that permission would not be granted. It was left in the air, with the thought that if Fred had to go alone Joyce would follow as soon as she became of age. Fred was happy to go along with her suggestions, after all, who knew what would happen with a continent between them, it was difficult enough to maintain the relationship with only a few miles. He did wonder if it had been so much easier to express his "love" for Joyce and agree to her proposals knowing that he might be escaping soon, easier to run away than stay.

It had been a phone call from Tommy that had prompted thoughts of leaving the country. He'd only been gone a few days but it was obvious that he wasn't settling down to army life as easily as he'd thought he would. He was struggling to make new friends and missed his family and chums back home already. He was especially missing Daisy, they had had a very difficult conversation after he had told her he was signing up. Daisy was beside herself and couldn't understand why Tom had to volunteer, especially as he was the only one of the gang that was married. But as he explained to her, that was precisely why he was doing what he was doing. He was thinking of their future together, the future of their children, if and when they came along. It wasn't just about him any more he said, and he begged her to understand. Daisy did understand, when Tom put it like that, of course she did, but it didn't stop her heart breaking. The training was harder than he expected and the graphic tales of the war his sergeant insisted on telling the rookies, as the new recruits were known as, ostensibly to harden them up, had made Tom feel physically ill. The romantic notion of signing up and fighting for his country was rapidly losing its appeal as far as Tom was concerned and Fred couldn't help but feel the same. He knew that his mother wasn't keen for him to volunteer and although, initially, Fred had been very eager to do just that, now he wasn't so sure. The idea of starting a new life away from it all was extremely inviting, he hadn't spoken to his mother about it yet, that was a whole different conversation. He had no doubts at all that she would be reluctant to let him go, but he also knew that she would support his decision if it meant that he would be safe from this wretched war. Fred thought about Tom and how hopeful and confident he had been that last night in the pub, the future had seemed to be mapped out for them all one way or another, if only life were that simple. He decided he would discuss all the possibilities with his mother that evening. She had been the voice of reason throughout his life, ever since his father had abandoned his family when he and his brother were children, although his brother was much older than him. He didn't even know where his father was these days, birthday cards had been sporadic and then dried up completely and his mother didn't like to talk about it. She didn't talk much about his elder brother either, who had long left home but had kept in touch with their father and although his mother didn't entirely approve she understood the it had to be his choice. She had quite a cordial relationship with her eldest child now, as did Fred on the odd occasions that he saw him. Very little was said on the subject and It had just been the two of them for so long that Fred felt a chill at the thought of being parted from her, he also knew that she would not go with him if he left. Yes, it was going to be a difficult conversation, but a necessary one. And sooner rather than later.

Letter Twenty Four

68 St Andrews Rd
Cheltenham

Sunday

Dearest Fred

It's almost bed time now – but I promised I'd write tonight so I must at least start. Fact is I couldn't catch the post anyhow on Sunday. I haven't been to church for weeks and weeks so went with Rachel and father tonight. Somehow it affected me quite a lot. The atmosphere of a church or chapel is sufficient to make me feel different inside. At least me, perhaps you're not taken that way. After the service we had singing (choruses of well known hymns in with the soldiers next door). Daddy saw that I behaved myself – I only smiled sweetly and sang like a lark. I met a fellow I had known when I was quite a kiddie he's going to be a missionary in Portuguese West Africa. He walked home with daddy and Rachel and I and told us all about it. It was quite interesting. He strongly disapproves of cinemas. We had quite an argument on the subject. He failed to persuade me that there was any harm in them.

I was surprised to find how my attitude to life and religion had altered This fellow and I now have entirely different outlooks on life. We look to get different things out of it, and yet a few years ago we were kids at Sunday school together and had almost identical ideals and aims.

Funny isn't it? Still if I'd been like he is now I'd probably never have loved you – so you ought to be glad that I am as I am. It sounds quite grandmotherly doesn't it? It's not meant to be a sermon just the result of going to church and godly influence.

It was good to speak to you this morning dear. I hadn't heard your voice for so long. I though your suggestion of going to America was pretty good. I think you know that you would have had no need to doubt whether or not I would go – I'm sorry your job is so insecure.

Father offended me greatly at dinnertime, the family and aunt Rose and grandma were discussing marriage etc and daddy said you and I were not at all suited to each other, that we'd never be happy. I couldn't decide whether he was serious or not. He wouldn't explain anything about it. I was most indignant I just told them a few things. Anyway it's nothing to do with him is it? Perhaps you're not interested still you might let me know what you think on the subject.

I'm looking forward to a really nice letter from you dear. I'm glad you still love me, it's nice to have someone isn't it? All your very own. Well, my Fred I must go now will write again soon.

All my love

Joyce

Fred was quite alarmed when he read Joyce's letter that afternoon. Why did her father think they were such an unsuitable match? He thought it was an odd thing to say, and unlike Joyce, was pretty sure that he was serious, deadly serious. He wondered if Joyce had mentioned America, if she had even hinted at them going away together. He could easily understand why Mr Wright had been so convinced of their unsuitability, he would have felt exactly the same in his shoes. Besides which, it would make for a very uncomfortable visit if he did get to see her before Christmas.

In some respects Fred felt that Joyce's last letter had created a sort of catalyst, he had to make decisions, he felt under a great deal of strain which was a new experience for him, he needed to make his mind up about the future and he needed to do it as soon as possible. He had decided that he wasn't a brave man, something that came as quite a revelation to him, nevertheless he resolved to sit down and talk it through once again, with the one person he knew wouldn't judge him.

Even after a good long talk with his mother Fred still felt he was going round in circles. He was a very confused young man and no mistake. He decided, after much deliberation, that he would go and visit his elder brother George, that they hadn't seen much of each other over the last few years was a bit of a stumbling bloke, but Fred felt that he needed to talk to someone older and wiser, and also someone who had more experience in the affairs of the heart. Also, if going to America was even a remote possibility he had to know that there would someone around to look after his mother. He would have much preferred that she go with him, but he knew in his heart of hearts that she would never leave Coventry. That afternoon he popped into the tailor's shop where George worked, and hung around until his brother was free. Although George was extremely surprised to see him, he nevertheless agreed that they could meet up on Sunday morning and have a proper talk, it was impossible whilst he was working and he suggested Fred call at his home around 11am so that they could chat without interruptions.

When Fred told his mother of his plans she was surprisingly reasonable about it. In actual fact she felt it might be a very good idea. Her relationship with her eldest had never been a particularly close one, she had been very young when he was born, and didn't settle into motherhood well at all. Her husband had been very little help and she had been quite down in the dumps for some time following the birth. She found it much easier when Fred came along unexpectedly eleven years later and he quickly became her favourite which caused problems within the family, which she had had the grace to acknowledge. Unfortunately it caused a permanent rift between herself, her husband and her eldest boy, which had never been fully repaired.

But she also acknowledged that George was a bright, sensitive boy who had grown up to be a very rounded and sensible young man. She thought that Fred may actually get some very sound advice from him.

Letter Twenty Five

68 St Andrews Rd
Cheltenham

Thursday

My Dearest Fred

Thanks so much for your nice long letter. It was awfully nice to get such an epistle from you, I thought the tone rather conveyed the impression of a father talking to his little girl. I guess it was me demanding to be treated as an equal, also as the one and only girlfriend – not an infant. You seemed rather upset dearest by my letter, I assure you I didn't mean to worry you. I guess you took the whole matter more seriously than I did. Knowing my father, he often comes out with weird ideas. Mother is different, she approves of you because she thinks you're frightfully sensible and look after me – also you "boss me about" which mother says is very necessary.

Are you convinced that no-one has taken a disapproving attitude to you? I refuse to discuss the matter with either of them. After all it's my affair not theirs. Surely a person ought to know his or her own mind. If not they are pretty weak specimens. Matter closed. Finis.

May I add a little more on the subject – I was altered before I met you – it is generally attributed to the effect of the Post Office staff. My own candid opinion is that I just grew up and started thinking and acting on my own. Anybody would think that from being an awfully nice person I had degraded into the lowest of the low. You know quite well this is not so! It's the missionary fellow who has changed such a lot, not me. I agree with you that we'd get along pretty well, taking it for granted that we're normally intelligent. Two people who are fond of each other shouldn't find it hard to 'give a little' should they?

We get ourselves awfully entangled in questions and arguments which would probably never arise if we lived nearer each other, don't you agree? I think we'll have to buy an aeroplane when the war is over.

By the way I have started the pullover, it really is a work of art. It will probably take me quite a while to do as it's rather involved. I rather enjoy knitting something that one day you will have (I hope). The wool doesn't look at all bad knitted up, the female friends of mine that have seen the unfinished article think its pretty good.

It's frightfully cold here dearest – spent yesterday evening drinking coffee at the 'Royal Cinema'. Nothing exciting has happened for so long that I really forget the last thing of interest that happened around here.

Oh Fred dear do you remember those 'photos' you took of me at August, the one from which you had the enlargement done. All the relatives seem to have fallen for it and consider it their right to have one. I wonder if it is possible dear for you to get a few more done like that one?

I, like you, wish I had my boyfriend to go out for a walk with tonight. I'm afraid I shan't know what to say to him, I shall be out of practise – perhaps if I just kissed you nicely you'd be quite satisfied would you?

Lots of people seemed to think that Hitler was coming over Cheltenham for the races. He doesn't seemed to have arrived. We're frightfully disappointed.

Of course we've been pretty busy at work. I understand that you are going to visit your brother on Sunday morning so I shan't ring you until Sunday night. Fred dear I do wish you could manage to come down for a weekend. I suppose the prospect of a Monday morning off is pretty hopeless. It's disquieting to have you miles away – while I just get fed up here. It somehow doesn't seem to worry you – still I mustn't grumble I have still got you even if you are just a little way away. By the way you didn't tell me that you still love me – do you?

Must go now darling to catch the post

All my love

Your own

Joyce

It had been quite a productive Sunday morning with George, he had been surprisingly understanding, although he thoroughly disapproved of Fred's idea about going to America instead of joining the navy as he had previously suggested. 'Running away' he called it, much to Fred's shame. Otherwise he was very supportive. He told Fred that he didn't think the age gap was anything to worry about, lots of girls married older men and usually the relationship was the stronger for it. When all was said and done, the only two people that really mattered were himself and Joyce and whether they really loved each other. If their love was strong enough, and if that was the case then they would find a way to overcome any obstacles. But, said George, there was a war on after all and nothing was going to be easy. Not for them or for anybody else, but, life had to go on regardless and they should grasp any chance of happiness they could.

Fred came away from the visit marginally more lighthearted than he had been when he arrived.

He read through Joyce's letter again, he was sorry she felt that he had been a little condescending, he hadn't meant to address her as if she were a child, indeed, he hadn't realised he had until he thought about it. He had been disappointed by her father's comments but Joyce couldn't say it wasn't their affair when it most definitely was. Joyce's parent's obviously thought of her still as an innocent young lady, well her father definitely did, her mother was a little more liberal minded.

Her letter was quite hard to follow actually, she did jump from subject to subject. In fact she wrote in the same way that she talked. For once though, a lot of what she had said made sense. The fact of the matter was that she had grown up. Even since they had first met she had changed, matured, started taking life more seriously, beginning to be the practical one, it was one of the things he loved about her. There was that word again, Fred had been remiss not to tell her he loved her in his last letter, he didn't even know why. Except, how do you really know, how do you judge it, what makes one relationship so different from another? Fred was beginning to feel that he was the child and Joyce the grown up, which wouldn't do at all.

Fred folded up the letter and got ready to go out. Joyce was phoning in an hour and then he was off to Ma Cooper's to have a pint, or two, with Bob and Maurice. He would make sure he was especially kind to Joyce when they spoke, also, he was curious to know why on earth the good folk of Cheltenham had thought Hilter might be visiting the racecourse!

Letter Twenty Six

68 St Andrews Rd
Cheltenham

Monday

Dearest Fred

Thanks for your letter which I received this morning. I'm awfully sorry to hear that you have a cold. Lingering about in the cold night air I suppose? I think it was awfully nice of you to write such a nice long letter, it must have taken you ages – I'm glad you love me enough to spend such a long time on my correspondence. Also the ink is very superior. I've been doing some thinking (most unusual I agree) and I've come to the conclusion that I can get two days leave.

The days are those following Xmas more precisely. I shall probably be off Xmas itself; work boxing day and the next day and then have two days leave (if I wanted them).

By rapid thinking I came to the conclusion that you would probably have a week's holiday following the Xmas festivities themselves, is this so? If so you could spend Xmas with your people and then come down to Cheltenham for a few days. Of course if you don't get the leave its pretty hopeless but if you can it would be rather a good idea wouldn't it? I hope you don't mind me putting the idea forward but somehow I'm of the opinion that it doesn't matter much which of us makes the suggestion – although it may not appear ladylike or maidenly. I don't think I aspire to the latter and the former seems quite a hard job.

I worked on Sunday in the morning and went to Stroud in the afternoon to see a girl – friend (actually more acquaintance than friend) who is going to London on Tuesday. Her people are old friends of the family and were very fussy, etc. I then returned home the soul occupant of the bus – stayed at home the remainder of the evening knitting (your pullover) so that mother could go to church. Elsie and I had roast chestnuts which she roasted over the fire and made a filthy mess all over the hearth, the rug, and us.

Returning to the subject of you – I must really reprimand you for getting morbid, you know quite well I don't allow it about you? I don't agree with you that the hurt exceeds the happiness, after all the hurt is sent to prove the happiness, don't you agree? If everything always went smoothly, one would not appreciate the beauty of life it would become monotonous, boring, commonplace. I'm still of the opinion that I can deliver good sermons. I wonder if you'd listen to me if I tried to talk to you in such a way. Your superior age makes it possible for you to have the upper hand. I think perhaps you'd have to be the boss. How would that suit you? You'd be nice to me wouldn't you dear?

Mother has just interrupted to say she sends her love – also hopes to see you around about Christmas so see what you can do infant won't you? It will take me ages to knit your pullover it's an awful long time growing.

Must really go now I shall try to ring you up tomorrow but it will probably not be possible.

Must go now.

Lots of love

Your own

Joyce

Fred's Mother was starting to seriously worry about him. It was unlike him to be so indecisive, he was normally so level headed and she had been hoping that his talk with George would have helped, but he still seemed to be in a quandary. At least he had definitely decided that

America was out of the question and the navy was the next step, which worried her even more. What was it her own mother used to say? "A mother is only as happy as her unhappiest child!" He had gone to work that morning like he had the weight of the world on his shoulders. Something really needed to happen to shake him out of it, and about two o'clock that afternoon it did.

Normally personal phone calls weren't allowed at the office so Fred was surprised and a little alarmed to be told that there was a call for him in the outer office. He picked up the phone with some trepidation, it was Tom's brother Harry, Tom had been in an accident and was badly hurt. It transpired that a section had left the barracks the previous evening to take baths, as they marched to the wash rooms a heavy goods vehicle had ploughed into the back of them. There should have been a solider walking behind carrying a red lamp but for some reason he hadn't been on duty and the truck simply hadn't seen them in time. By all accounts Tom was one of the lucky ones in that he survived, two other chaps had been killed outright and several others injured like Tom. His right leg had been shattered by the impact and he was now in the hospital. Sadly it was possible that he might lose his leg, one thing was sure said Harry, his fighting days were definitely over – he would never see any action now.

Fred was stunned by the news, Tom was his best and oldest friend. Good hearted and true, he was everything you could wish for in a pal, an all round good egg. He spent the rest of the afternoon in a daze, on the one hand grateful that Tom had survived, but also imagining how he would have felt had Tom died. The idea that he might have lost such a dear friend, never to have seen him again, sent a chill through him.

By the time clocking off came round Fred had done a lot of thinking. Tom's accident had shocked him greatly, which somehow had the effect of clearing his head. For the first time in a long time Fred realised how you knew if you were in love. Tom had been like a brother to him, always there when he needed him, especially throughout the difficult times when his relationship with George was almost nonexistent. He realised that he loved Tom with all his heart, even if it wasn't considered a very manly thing to confess to and now he also knew without any doubt at all that he loved Joyce. The idea of something happening to her, and never being able to see her again filled him with dread. This is how you know, he thought, when you can't imagine life without them, when your world becomes nothing if they are not in it. When they are the other half of your heart beat. He had been a fool and no mistake. It was time to grab the bull by the horns and act!

The phone call to Joyce's office was a little bit awkward, he knew, as in his own workplace, that personal calls were frowned upon. To top it all, Joyce wasn't at work as she was on the late shift. Fred managed to persuade the supervisor on shift to put him through to Colin, the chap that used to put the calls through for Joyce. Could he please tell her, the moment she arrived, that he had a very important question to ask her and it couldn't wait, not even for a day, could she please let him know as soon as possible when she could phone him, he knew she was working late but didn't mind how late she called. Just as long as she did.

Colin promised to pass on the message and smiled knowingly to himself as he hung up.

As soon as Fred got home that afternoon he told his mother about the recent events and that he had finally made up his mind, and also that he was absolutely sure it was the right decision. Fred's mother was delighted, she could already see, even in light of Tom's accident, how much happier he was. They sat drinking tea, wondering how Joyce would let him know when she could call, they didn't have to wait very long. There was a knock at the door just after six o'clock. It was a Post Office telegram. It read as follows:

DEAREST FRED – STOP

WILL CALL YOU AT EIGHT PM THIS EVENING – STOP

I LOVE YOU – STOP

Twenty Six Letters

Milton Keynes UK
Ingram Content Group UK Ltd.
UKHW021002101023
430299UK00006B/418